Play Me A Tale

Play Me A Tale

T.L. Stevens

ISBN: 979-8-9917568-1-5 (e-book)
ISBN: 979-8-9917568-0-8 (paperback)

Library of Congress Control Number: 2024921866

Printed in the United States of America

Dedication

This book is dedicated to both my paternal grandma and maternal grandma, for all the treasured memories they left me with. Of course, the more time I spent with them the more cherished memories I have. Now, being a grandma myself, I love to spend as much time with my grandkids as possible. My hope is they will have lots of fond memories of all the adventures we had together. Memories that will live on long after I'm gone.

I also want to thank all my readers, especially those who've taken the time to leave a rating or review and referred my books to others. I appreciate and value your feedback.

Table of Contents

Moving Day

Nina ran through the small condo using the multiple stacks of boxes as secret hideouts from whatever was chasing her. With her overactive imagination, it was anyone's guess. Whatever foe she was fleeing from kept her on the run. Nina's voice echoed through the space filling it with childhood fun and creativity. Her mom and grandma couldn't help but join in her excitement as she raced back into the living room announcing she had found a treasure map.

"A treasure map?" asked her mom, "Where did you find it?"

Nina's voice reached an all-time high pitch as she explained, "Someone slipped it under the front door and I grabbed it from them."

"You are very fast," commented Grandma, "Would you show it to us?"

Nina held the piece of paper close to her chest and carefully looked around to make sure her adversary wasn't lurking about. She finally agreed to show them the map. Moving in close to her mom and grandma she cautiously revealed the treasure map. She was right about one thing, it was a map, a map of the condo complex. It showed where trash bins were located as well as the office, the dog park, guest parking and so much more.

With a whisper Nina said, "I'm going to go look for the treasure," and with that she crept away.

Nina's mother, Valerie, shared her thoughts with her mom, "She reminds me so much of Grandma."

"Yes she does. She would have loved her great-grandma. It breaks my heart they never met."

Valerie could see the sadness well up in her mom's eyes as Theresa remembered her mother. Valerie had her own cherished memories of her grandma, far too many to count. One of the things she loved most about her grandma was her creativity, which brought Valerie full circle to her daughter. Nina had inherited her great-grandma's talent for make-believe. It didn't matter where they were or if Nina had a toy with her, she always found a way to turn any place into a fantasy world.

It wasn't until Valerie and her mother broke for lunch did Nina make another appearance and that was only because they called for her. Nina's dirty, smudge covered face proved she was working hard at finding the treasure. Little did she know it was only a matter of time before she found one.

Before they finished their lunch, there was a knock on the door. To Theresa's delight it was the remainder of her belongings. They had packed as many of the smaller and lighter boxes into Valerie's SUV that they could, leaving the heavy stuff for the movers. Whose late arrival was explained by the fact that their truck had broken down. The sight of her bed arriving made Theresa smile. Her aching body was looking forward to climbing into bed and getting a good night's sleep.

Nina was excited about more obstacles to hide behind or work through. Both her grandma and mom saw lots of work ahead, while Nina saw towering trees, caves to explore and even an island she could pretend to swim around. Nina's ability to get lost in her imaginary worlds sometimes proved to be a problem, especially in school and with homework. However, even with all her daydreaming Nina managed to get good grades. At times amusing her mom, especially when Nina used her pretending to help her with her homework.

Nina was getting antsy on the floor, but Valerie kept her daughter from venturing off into her make-believe world by reminding her, "You need to finish your lunch before you can go back to playing."

Nina gulped down her milk before she finished chewing to keep from choking on the huge bite of pizza in her mouth. In no time, she had fine-tuned the process and Nina was done long before the movers where finished. She tossed her paper plate & napkin in the trash and was ready to run off to play. Grandma stepped in to offer some assistance with keeping Nina out of the mover's way, "Nina, would you help me unpack some of my keepsakes?"

"What are keepsakes?" questioned Nina stopping in her tracks.

"They are things that belonged to my mom, your great-grandma. They are very old and meant an awful lot to her. So, I keep them safe and sound in this box. Someday I will pass them down to your mom and you."

Nina wasn't sure it sounded like much fun, especially since there was a whole new world of things and places to explore in Grandma's new home. Valerie knew her daughter needed a bit more encouragement and perhaps some gentle direction, "It'll be fun Nina you'll see. Besides you need to stay out of the way of the movers."

With a humph Nina plopped down on the floor. A disapproving look from Valerie was enough to correct Nina's attitude. Carefully Valerie opened the well taped box. One by one she handed its contents to Theresa who was seated on the only folding chair they had. There were pictures of Nina's distant family members, none of which she knew and several of her great-grandma with Theresa as a young lady. The number of photos seemed never ending and other than her grandma everyone else were strangers. Just when Nina's mind began to wander something caught her eye.

A miniature gold piano was slowly and gently pulled from layers of bubble wrap. The little grand piano was beautiful, but that was just the beginning. Grandma told Nina it was also a music box. The gold legs and sides were covered with pretty little details. All the edges were lined with golden ropes making it look like it was tied together. There were tiny delicate swirls etched into the golden sides and bottom of the piano. The legs looked like upside down ice cream cones with the scoop of ice cream being smashed nearly flat by the weight of the piano. Placing the piano on a large box showed how steady it was on its legs.

Nina laughed while she said, "That's what happened to the ice cream."

Both Theresa and Valerie were confused, so Nina showed them how the legs looked like ice cream cones with a flattened scoop of ice cream at the bottom. This made them all laugh. "You have quite the imagination," boasted Grandma.

"Yes I do, I'm really good at pretending," agreed Nina without a hint of arrogance.

With a chuckle Valerie recalled a memory of how Nina once used a litter of puppies to complete her second-grade math homework. They weren't real puppies, actually they were odd items she gathered from the kitchen's junk drawer, but in Nina's eyes they were puppies. As each puppy found a new home Nina was able to complete her math homework with 100% accuracy.

"I do remember that story," commented Grandma. "You have always been very smart jellybean." It was the affectionate term Theresa came up with when Nina ate her first jellybean. An amused Theresa giggled as her granddaughter made an adorably cute sour face. Theresa had warned Nina she probably wouldn't like the candy, but saying it was sour didn't mean much to a three-year-old.

Nina smiled at her grandma calling her jellybean. That loving pet name was theirs and theirs alone. Nina's eyes refocused on the miniature piano. "Is it a toy?"

"No jellybean, it's a music box."

"Oh, yeah. I forgot," admitted Nina. "What does it play?"

Theresa and Valerie shared a sorrowful look. "Grandma's music box stopped playing music a long time ago," explained Valerie.

"So the piano is yours Grandma?" Nina asked.

Theresa smiled realizing Nina only had one living grandma, so she did her best to explain, "Nina we all have moms. You have your mom," pointing to Valerie, "and your mom has a mom and that's me," she said placing her hand on her chest. "I too had a mom but she's not alive anymore. Her name was Ruth; she is your great-grandma and the piano was hers."

Nina glanced at her mom then her grandma and simply replied, "That's a lot of mom's," and then she jumped to her next question, "Can we fix the piano?"

"We tried that, but no one has been able to fix it," answered Valerie.

Theresa turned the piano over while Nina tried to convince her mom to try one more time to have the music box fixed. Theresa took hold of the winding key and ever so gently tried to turn it, but as expected it didn't give way. Not wanting to damage the piano Theresa didn't force the winding key to turn.

Nina and Nina alone heard the faintest sound. She shouted with joyful excitement, "I heard something! The music box made a sound. Didn't you hear it?"

Just then one of the movers came in singing along to the music coming from the small portable radio he had sat on top of the box he was carrying. Nina's face sank. She thought for sure the sound had come from the little piano.

A Promise Made

Brokenhearted over being wrong Nina finished her milk, threw her paper cup in the trash and asked if she could go play. The movers weren't quite finished so Valerie instructed her to stay in the living room so she wouldn't be in the way.

"How about the patio?" negotiated Nina.

Valerie took a peek at the walled in patio and agreed. It wasn't long before Nina's laughter reached their ears. Curious as to how she was having so much fun prompted her mom and grandma to spy on her. Seated on the ground was Nina using leaves that had fallen from an overhanging tree as people. They were having quite the conversation. As a twig fell towards Nina she imagined it was a pterodactyl. The leaf people ran for cover hiding in the single potted plant tucked in the far corner of the patio.

"She sure does take after Grandma," replied Valerie with a smile.

Theresa nodded in agreement, "I can't even imagine the fun those two would have had. Between Mom and Nina's inventiveness there would be no end to the fascinating stories and adventures they would have come up with."

Nina heard the mover's say they were leaving. Now it was time to go explore the make-believe world waiting for her inside. She rushed into the condo and her eyes were drawn to the piano which Grandma had sat on the kitchen counter. While the movers and Grandma took care of paperwork, Nina found herself staring at the beautiful piano. With her elbows on the counter she rested her face in her hands examining the painting on the piano lid. Moving in as close as she could she noticed there was a man pushing a woman on a tree swing. The fallboard had a painting of swans swimming in a pond. Upon further investigation Nina caught sight of various animals hiding in the lid's painting. There were birds and squirrels in the trees, rabbits under the bushes and a deer hiding behind the large tree that the woman's swing was tied to. Nina also spotted fish in the pond below the swans and a frog along the bank.

Her curiosity grew when she discovered several more animals doing their best to hide, but when she noticed a butterfly gracefully fly across the scene on the lid's painting she was captivated. "Hello little butterfly. Where you going?"

"Who are you talking to jellybean?"

Nina refused to pull her eyes away from the piano but still answered, "The pretty butterfly flying around on top of the piano."

"Did a butterfly get in the house?" asked Valerie.

Still focused on the piano Nina calmly replied, "No mom, it's in the painting."

Both Grandma and Mom walked over to take a look. Grandma didn't see the butterfly until she put her glasses on, but Valerie spotted it right away. It had stopped flying when they approached, but neither of them remembered noticing it before. Valerie simply said, "I guess I never looked at it that close."

Theresa agreed, "Me neither, but it was usually Mom who wound up the music box before she played with me."

That simple exchange brought back a memory neither of them had thought about in years. Theresa looked at her daughter and granddaughter, smiled with tears in her eyes and said, "Play me a tale."

Valerie's eyes lit up and they shared a fond look of a long forgotten memory. Nina broke their gaze by asking, "Play me a tale? What's that mean?"

Valerie answered, "It means play me a story, tale is another word for story."

Grandma went on to explain. "My mom, had this piano for as long as I can remember. It's been passed down through our family for generations so it is very old. Not only is it old, but it used to be magical."

"Magical?" Nina was now completely tuned in to the conversation and wanted to know all there was to know.

Grandma appeared to be both happy and sad at the same time when she explained her magical comment. "Well, I used to believe it was magical when I was a little girl. So, did your mom when she was little."

"Why?" questioned Nina wanting to know so much more than what was being said.

The memory of days gone by was making it tough for Theresa to speak. Valerie stepped in. "My grandma, your great-grandma liked to play pretend as much, if not more than you do Nina. She would wind up the music box and let it play while she told me wonderful stories of princess's, dragons, flying people...."

Theresa broke in, "My favorite were the tales about talking animals."

"Oh yes. Those were some of my favorite stories," agreed Valerie.

Nina wondered something. "Why did she play the music box when she told you stories?"

Excitement bubbled from Theresa, "That's the magical part jellybean. When your great-grandma told me one of her made up stories they would come to life when the music played. Not only was I listening to the stories it felt like I was there. It was a dream come true playing with my mom."

Nina's eyes lit up. This all sounded too good to be true and yet something inside Nina believed it to be true. The look of pure joy on her mom's face strengthened her belief. "You too Mom?"

"Yes. Some of the best times in my life were spent with Grandma Ruth. There was always an adventure to go on. Grandma never seemed to run out of stories and if she ever repeated a story it only got better," Valerie replied.

To Theresa and Valerie's surprise Nina didn't say a word for minutes. She was clearly deep in thought or more likely inside her world of imagination. When she did finally speak, it wasn't what either of them were expecting. "Why don't you guys tell stories like Great-Grandma?"

Grandma answered, "I never had my mom's imagination. Her gift of pretending skipped me," Theresa paused and looked over at her daughter, then with sadness in her voice Valerie added, "and me too."

In an effort to lighten the mood Valerie pointed out, "It didn't skip you Nina. You are very much like your Great-Grandma Ruth."

That little tidbit made all of them smile and in no time, they were back to unpacking all that needed to be unpacked for the day. The bed was made, dishes, cups and silverware found their homes and of course the coffee maker was ready to go for the morning. When darkness fell, it became clear that lamps needed to be found and plugged in. The single overhead light fixtures in the kitchen, bathroom and bedroom wasn't enough to light up the place, especially with Grandma's failing eyesight.

Nina had fallen asleep on the floor behind stacks of boxes in the living room. Valerie gently woke her daughter and told her they needed to get home. Nina was looking forward to seeing her dad. He had left early to go fishing with a visiting friend so she hadn't seen him all day.

With a hug and a kiss Nina said good-bye to her grandma. Then she gathered the crayons and coloring books she'd brought with her. Looking down at the coloring book on top of the pile brought her back to Great-Grandma's music box. The cover of the book had a brightly colored butterfly on it. She could envision the butterfly flying across the lid of the piano. Nina couldn't help herself, "Grandma could I take the music box home?"

Valerie cut in, "Nina you're too young to have that just yet. Besides it belongs to Grandma." She was a little disappointed her daughter was asking for something that meant so much to her grandma.

Nina defended her question, "I'm almost nine and half, I'm not too young," using her mom's words. It was a rare occasion that Nina ever questioned her mom, but her stance proved she was determined.

Maintaining control but speaking in a firm tone Valerie responded, "First, you turned nine two months ago. Secondly, the music box is not a toy Nina, it's a keepsake that has been passed down through the family because it's always been very well taken care of."

"I'll take care of it."

"And if it somehow gets broken? Do you want to be the one in the family that breaks the music box?"

"No, but....."

Theresa added some calmness to the debate, "Let's look at this carefully, shall we?" She didn't want to step on Valerie's toes when it came to raising her daughter, but perhaps there was a way to work this out. "Let's see if we can agree on a compromise."

"Compromise?" Nina questioned.

"Yes a compromise. It means to find a way to make both of you a little happy without either of you getting exactly what you want," explained Theresa in a way Nina would understand. "The music box is supposed to be passed down and it is already broken, at least the music box part, but the rest of it is in perfect condition. So, what if I give it to your mom and she keeps it safely in her bedroom? That way you can see it whenever you want."

Nina looked at her mom who nodded in agreement to Theresa's suggestion. "I think that would be a nice compromise, but are you sure you don't want to keep it a bit longer Mom?" Valerie asked.

"This place is much tinier than my house. I'm not sure I'll have room for all my stuff once I get everything unpacked."

"Well, if you think it's a good idea I'll agree to it."

"Good," said Theresa, who then turned her focus to Nina, "Jellybean I want you to promise you won't touch or pick up the music box without your mom. None of us want to see it get broken any more than it already is. Do you promise?"

"I promise Grandma," replied Nina standing tall and placing her hand across her chest.

"Very well. I believe we have found a compromise."

Before opening the door to leave Nina gave her grandma another huge hug. "Thank you Grandma."

"You're very welcome jellybean. If you keep your promise and I know you will, I will keep my promise."

"What's your promise Grandma?" a curious Nina asked.

"On your tenth birthday I will ask your mom to move the music box from her room to yours. I was ten when your great-grandma put the music box in my room, so I think you'll be ready to have it in your room."

Valerie had all but forgotten that she was also ten when she was allowed to put the music box in her room. When Valerie got married and moved away she left it behind knowing her mom needed it more than she did. Valerie's father had passed away a little over a month before her wedding making her big day bittersweet. Taking the music box away from her mom at that time would have only added to Theresa's pain. Emotions ran high when Valerie hugged her mom good-bye. They were both remembering why Theresa still had the music box.

Waving goodbye Nina hollered, "I'll keep my promise Grandma!"

Sweet Dreams

Nina had a hard time going to bed that night. She knelt on her parent's bed staring at the music box. It had been placed on top of her dad's dresser. She knew her mom had picked his dresser because it was too tall for her to reach.

"It's time for bed," Nina's dad reminded her.

"Just a few more minutes, please," begged Nina.

Her dad smiled at her, she knew Dad gave in more often than Mom. "We're locking up downstairs, but when we're done you better be in your bed." She had gotten her way, but she also knew that if she let her dad down and didn't do as he said he wouldn't give in so easily next time.

"I will."

When Nina heard the footsteps of her parents starting up the stairs, she was thankful she was already in her pj's. She hopped off the bed and headed for the door. That's when she heard a single note come from the music box. How she wanted to turn around and glance at the music box, but her parent's voices were getting closer. Darting down the hallway she jumped onto her bed and was doing her best to get under the blankets when Dad came into her room. He was confirming she had listened to him. Thankfully her light was off. She hadn't even bothered to turn it on as she raced towards her bed. If he noticed her wiggling to get under the covers he didn't say so.

"Good night angel," he said with a kiss on her forehead. Marc began calling his daughter angel from the first-time he held her in his arms. As far as he was concerned that's exactly what she looked like.

Mom had entered the room and wished Nina goodnight in her own special way. She wrapped her in a big hug, kissed her cheek saying "A squeeze and a kiss to take with you to dreamland."

With a smile Nina squeezed her mom back. Valerie savored the moment. She knew there would come a time when Nina would no longer enjoy their bedtime ritual as much as she did. Just before Valerie shut the door she whispered, "Sweet dreams."

Nina rolled over on her side and just above a whisper replied, "Always, Mama." It was one of the rare times Nina called her mom that, it was her own special goodnight wish. Closing her eyes Nina found herself lost in thinking about the music box and her great-grandma and how she wished she had gotten to know her. Remembering a photo from earlier that day of her great-grandma feeding a horse an apple led Nina straight into an amazingly wonderful dream.

Nina swung on great-grandma's swing set trying to get higher and higher with each kick of her legs. Great-Grandma Ruth was busy hanging clothes on the line under the large apricot tree in her backyard. The smell of homemade chicken soup floated on the breeze and when Nina inhaled the mouthwatering aroma it made her stomach growl. Jumping from the swing as it reached the highest point Nina landed with a "Woohoo!"

"Did you jump off the swing?"

With a prideful smile Nina answered, "Yes I did. I learned how to do it at school."

"Good job!" clapped great-grandma before picking up the now empty laundry basket.

"I'm hungry Gram." Nina had never used that word, but it seemed the perfect fit for Great-Grandma Ruth.

"I think the soup is ready. Let's go in."

Nina skipped next to Gram for a moment, then she ran as fast as she could, beating Gram to the house. She knew the drill and headed straight for the bathroom to wash up. When she returned, Gram had already placed bowls of soup on the table with warm buttered biscuits. Gram asked, "What would you like to drink?"

"Lemonade please," replied Nina who then asked, "When I'm tall enough, can I wash my hands in the kitchen sink like you do?"

"Sure sweets," answered Gram. It warmed Nina's heart to be called sweets by her great-grandma.

Just then a neighbor's cat wandered into the house. He jumped up on an empty chair and asked, "Could I have a bowl of soup? The smell of your cooking has made me hungrier than normal."

Gram smiled and said, "Of course you can Tiger."

His owner had given the cat a very appropriate name. The large orange striped tabby looked like a miniature tiger. Nina quickly got up to grab a napkin and spoon for their visitor. "Here you go Tiger."

"Thank you Nina. I'm so glad you came to visit. Perhaps we could play a game after lunch."

"I would like that. How about a game of chase the feather?"

Tiger's eyes lit up. "I've been working on my leaping and I'll be able to catch the feather on the teaser wand no matter how high you put it."

"We'll see about that," taunted Nina with a playful smile.

Gram placed the soup in front of Tiger who leaned over to take a whiff. "MMMMM," he said as he was ready to lap up some of the broth. Gram cleared her throat reminding him to use his spoon. He could get away with eating like a normal cat everywhere else but at Gram's house. He picked up the spoon and said, "Shall we?"

When all three were done with lunch, Nina took her and Tiger's bowls to the sink and rushed off to find the cat toy. In no time, they were playing and laughing. Nina stood on the couch to hold the feather higher and out of reach, so Tiger jumped from the back of the couch saying, "I can still get it," and sure enough he did, pulling the wand from Nina's hand. Laughing loudly Nina fell backwards on the couch and was soon joined by Tiger. He laughed while climbing on top of her, stretching out across Nina's tummy he waited to be petted. She stroked the happy cat as he rolled from one side to the next saying, "Now this side," in between his purring. When they heard the sound of his owner calling for him, Tiger cleverly said, "Thank you for a purrfect afternoon," then he ran out the backdoor like any other cat.

"Did you and Tiger have fun?" Gram questioned.

"We sure did. I still don't understand how he can use a spoon without any thumbs," commented Nina.

"It's magical," was all Gram said.

Thankfully the magic wasn't over. In flew several nightingales and one of them asked, "How about some music?"

Gram walked over to the piano and said, "That's a splendid idea."

As Gram played song after song the birds chirped and whistled along. Before they knew it a pair of mice from the backyard sang the words of each song and soon they were joined by bunnies, squirrels and even an out of tune muskrat. The music filled the house and before Nina realized what was happening everything was shrinking. Everything that is except for the piano. The piano was now massive in size and had changed from Gram's upright piano into her golden music box piano.

The piano dwarfed them as they continued to get smaller and smaller. Music began to play from the golden piano making the animals flee.

Gram and Nina covered their ears. The sound was far too loud. Nina yelled, "Make it stop!"

Gram shrugged her shoulders and hollered, "I don't know how!"

The music increased in volume making them want to flee as well. That's when they noticed they had somehow ended up on top of Gram's coffee table. There was no way for them to get down. That's when Tiger came to their rescue. He jumped on the table then laid down so the two of them could climb aboard. Wrapping their arms tightly around his collar they firmly held on. After reminding them to hang on with all their might Tiger jumped from the table and rushed into the backyard. The yard looked so different from the never before seen vantage point.

Tiger laid down so they could climb off. "I'm so glad I came back for a second bowl of the soup."

"Me too," replied Gram.

"What happened?" Nina asked. Being so small frightened her and fearing there was no way to return to their normal size she began to cry.

Just then a large raven landed nearby. This only added to Nina's fear. Gram held her tight and was about to yell something at the towering bird, but the bird spoke first. "I'm here to help you." He bowed before them and whispered, "Please trust me."

Gram wasn't sure what to make of it and Tiger appeared to feel the same way. He stood over top of them shielding them from the raven. "Why should we trust you?" questioned Tiger.

The raven looked to the sky and shouted, "Sunnee would you help me?"

No sooner did the raven ask did a large yellow and orange butterfly flutter down from above. The butterfly was beautiful and exactly like the one Nina had seen fly across the lid of the music box. That's when Nina and Gram noticed they looked like painted people and so did everything around them.

"Come on, let's get you two home," muttered the butterfly in the sweetest voice they had ever heard. Sunnee laid on the ground flattening her wings out as much as she could, then she instructed them to climb up her wings and sit down on her back. They didn't feel the need to question her and immediately did as she asked. By the time they reached her back they were covered in yellow and orange powder making them sneeze. Sunnee flitted into the air and landed on the tip of a single blade of grass while saying, "Hold on, Sable wants to get you home. You've had quite a day."

It didn't take long for them to realize that Sable was the name of the raven. With terror filled eyes they watched as Sable opened his wings directly above Sunnee covering the three of them before enclosing them in his wings. Sunnee fluttered back to the ground and quickly asked Gram and Nina to slide down one of her wings adding, "If you don't move now I'll be crushed under you."

In no time, they began to grow bigger. Sable slowly opened his wings as they grew too large to be shielded by him. Sunnee made her escape only to return when they were their normal size. Nina held out her hand allowing Sunnee to land on her finger. Sable looked up at them saying, "I'm happy to help."

Gram apologized for not trusting him, prompting Nina to do the same. With a tone of sadness in his voice Sable admitted, "I'm used to it," making them feel even worse. With Sunnee still on her finger Nina squatted down and brushed her other hand along Sable's back. Her tender smile warmed his heart and he couldn't help but say, "Thank you Nina. That helps," and with that, both he and Sunnee flew away.

Nina giggled as they flew out of sight. Sunnee was right, it had been quite the day.

Nina woke to the sound of her own laughter. As she sat up in bed her dad came into the room. "What's so funny angel?"

"Oh I just had the best dream ever," Nina answered smiling from ear to ear.

"I can hardly wait to hear all about it, but we need to get ready to go help Grandma finish unpacking."

"Okay," replied Nina rather surprised it was already morning. The dream hadn't felt long enough to last all night, but she was thankful she had woken up when she did, because the remarkably special dream was still so vivid in her mind.

Friends Old and New

With Dad's help the rest of the unpacking went quickly. Everyone was so busy getting Grandma settled in they failed to notice Nina sitting on the floor in a corner of the living room going through an old photo album. She studied every detail captured by the camera, soaking in all she could. Her eyes lit up when she turned the page and there was Gram standing under the apricot tree in her backyard. Gram was younger than she had been in Nina's dream, but she could tell it was her.

"Whatcha looking at jellybean?" Grandma questioned.

With remembrance clouding her eyes Nina looked up and said, "I'm looking at Gram."

"Gram?"

"That's what I'm calling your mom," explained Nina, adding "I mean my great-grandma."

Clearly Nina had understood her grandma's explanation as to who her great-grandma was. The unusual look on Nina's face didn't go unnoticed. "Why do you look sad?"

"I'm sad I never got to meet her, but I visited with her in my dream last night."

Grandma's eyes welled with tears as she hugged Nina. "I'm sorry you didn't get to meet her, but I'd like to hear more about you dreaming of her."

By this time both of Nina's parents had joined them. All the work was done, so they took a seat. Nina sat on the couch with the photo album opened to Gram in her yard. It was the perfect way to start the story of her dream. She began telling them, in exceptional detail, about playing on the swing set and Gram hanging her laundry. Unfortunately, before she got to their lunch with Tiger and all the magic Theresa's doorbell rang. Grandma returned after a brief moment. Valerie smiled fondly at her mom and asked a rhetorical question, "Isn't youth wonderful?"

Theresa still moved by Nina's dream simply nodded yes. With love filling her eyes, she squeezed her granddaughter until Nina said she couldn't breathe. The room filled with laughter over Nina's words giving them all a much-needed emotional release. Dad lifted Nina into his arms and said, "You truly are my angel," then he placed a loving kiss on her forehead.

Grandma fixed one of Nina's favorite meals for all their help, complete with homemade tortillas. Nina stood mesmerized by her grandma's skill in rolling out the tortillas. Her grandma's hands seemed to dance with the well-worn French style rolling pin while rolling and flipping the tortillas in a rhythmic unison. As Grandma removed the last tortilla from the cast iron skillet she announced, "Dinner is served."

During dinner Nina asked question after question about Gram. She learned Gram had immigrated from Spain with her parents before she turned one. She had traveled in a covered wagon as a child, worked on her parent's farm feeding the animals as she grew and never learned to drive. Gram would walk into town for her errands and either take a bus or train for longer trips. Valerie smiled as she shared how she would go with her grandma on her nightly walks. Memories of Gram filled the room and Nina was all too happy to absorb everything she could.

Nina yawned, giving away just how tired she was. Nina fell asleep on the way home, sleeping so deeply she didn't make a sound when her dad placed her in her bed. The bright summer sun soon rose above the large tree outside Nina's bedroom bursting into her room. The radiant sunbeams hit her directly in the face. Nina squinted her eyes tightly and rolled over. The smell of pancakes and bacon nudged her awake. She sat up in bed feeling hungry; however, her hunger was quickly replaced with sadness. She hadn't dreamt of Gram all night.

"Good morning," greeted Valerie when Nina came down stairs.

"Good morning," replied Nina with a raspy voice.

"Are you hungry?"

Nina climbed onto the dining table bench with a nod. She looked around and asked, "Where's Dad?"

"He's at work," Valerie answered. "Summer break makes it a little hard to keep track of what day it is," she said smiling. Valerie fixed Nina a plate of food noticing her daughter was unusually quiet. Placing her food in front of Nina she questioned, "Are you feeling okay?"

"Yes. I just wish I had another dream about Gram last night."

"Well hang on to the one you did have," encouraged her mom before changing the subject, "What would you like to do today? There's nothing we have to get done, so you can pick what you want to do."

Nina thought long and hard. Without any siblings, she had learned to play by herself, but there were times she wanted to play with other kids. "Could Tiffany come over and play?"

"I'll call and ask her mom? Eat your breakfast and go get dressed. If Tiffany can play she'll want to get here as soon as possible."

From downstairs Valerie announced, "Tiffany can play, so make sure you make your bed."

With a newfound excitement Nina hollered, "It's already done."

"That's my girl!"

Within half an hour Tiffany arrived and after a quick hello she and Nina disappeared upstairs. Valerie being a clever mom chose to do laundry not only because it needed to be done, but it gave her a reason to make regular visits into Nina's room, especially if things were too quiet. Silence is normally a good thing, but when kids are involved silence can be suspicious. Thankfully and to be expected, the two girls were always found playing nicely in Nina's room.

Valerie took advantage of the quiet and plopped down on the couch to watch a little TV. Of course, that's when the girls came rushing down the stairs saying, "We're hungry." Valerie thought to herself, "It never fails." The girls ate their PB&J sandwiches outside on the patio and after licking their fingers clean of the cheesy mess from their chips they headed for the playset. They slid, swung, hung upside down on the monkey bars and played princess party in the playhouse. It wasn't until Valerie let the girls know that Tiffany's mom was on her way did Nina remember about the music box.

"Mom, can I show Tiffany Gram's piano?"

"Sure, I'll go get it."

Valerie set the piano on the dining table asking the girls not to touch it. Tiffany wanted to know if the keys worked, she actually took piano lessons. Before Valerie could answer Nina cut in, "No the keys don't work, but it used to play music. Only it's broken now," Nina's last few words sounded gloomy.

"Well it's very pretty," cheered Tiffany in an effort to brighten Nina's mood.

The two girls stared at the piano dissecting the details. Tiffany sort of bragged about knowing it was a miniature baby grand piano. While Tiffany went on to tell Nina far more than she cared to know about piano playing, Nina focused in on the beautiful butterfly she had seen fly around the painted top. This time the butterfly was frozen in place. Just then Nina spotted a large black bird coming from the top of the painting. It flew down towards the butterfly and together they flew off the edge of the painting. "Sable and Sunnee," whispered Nina so softly no one heard her. Nina then looked to see if they were flying on the side of the piano. There was nothing there so she once again turned her eyes back to the painting. Sable and Sunnee had not returned. That's when she noticed the bunnies hopping around the grass below the woman on the swing. Nina was happy the woman wasn't swinging, she was sure the bunnies would have been kicked.

"What are you staring at?" asked Tiffany.

Nina replied excitedly, "The bunnies."

Tiffany took a good long look. "Those are cute," was all she said.

Nina looked up at Tiffany wondering why she wasn't excited to see painted bunnies hopping around, but just like the butterfly the bunnies had stopped moving when someone else looked at the painting. Nina huffed and crossed her arms.

"Why are you mad?" Tiffany wondered. It was a rare occasion for Nina to be angry.

Nina was quick on her feet and said, "I'm not mad. I just wish I could hear the music it used to play." Nina wasn't sure Tiffany believed her but the arrival of her mom changed the subject. With a big hug the girls said goodbye and their moms planned a playdate at Tiffany's house near the end of the following week.

While Valerie began preparing dinner Nina took full advantage of Gram's music box being left on the dining table. Nina stared so long and hard at the painting searching for something, anything to move that her eyes began to blur. Valerie started setting the table remembering the piano was there. She carefully picked it up to take upstairs.

"Mom, I can take it upstairs," Nina offered.

"Thank you Nina but I'll do it."

"Can I touch it. Please. I'll be gentle."

Valerie realized Nina hadn't been allowed to touch the generational keepsake and that alone would make it more enticing. To help prevent Nina from doing something she shouldn't Valerie agreed. "I'll hold it and you can touch it."

With gentle fingers Nina ran them over the legs, then the fallboard before asking her mom to lift it up. Nina could feel the lines separating the tiny keys. Valerie was impressed by Nina's gentleness so she let her close the fallboard over the keys. At last she brushed her fingers ever so lightly across the painting on the piano lid. As Nina did this she felt something soft and fluffy. Looking down at the lid she noticed a bunny had filled the entire lid. The bunny nuzzled Nina's fingers with its head before hopping back into the painting taking the furry feeling with it.

The look of delight on Nina's face was a much bigger expression of happiness than Valerie expected for allowing Nina to touch the piano. Valerie wasn't sure why touching the piano had such an impact on her daughter, but she was thrilled it made her day.

Nina could hardly contain her excitement when she told her dad about her playdate with Tiffany. He too thought her excitement level over having her friend visit was a bit unusual and his glance towards Valerie showed they were in agreement. Later that evening Valerie shared with her husband the excitement Nina expressed over touching her great-grandma's musical piano. Even though Nina's excitement for the piano and Tiffany's visit was a bit over the top they were both pleased to see Nina so happy; chalking it up to the exuberant joys of childhood.

A Familiar Melody

Nina could hardly wait to be alone in her room. When Mom closed her bedroom door she picked up her favorite stuffed animal which just so happened to be a rabbit. It wasn't one of those cartoon-like bunnies. Instead it was a realistic brown bunny with a white chest, big dark brown eyes that resembled Nina's and a white fluffy tail. It reminded Nina of the bunny from the piano painting that had nuzzled her hand.

Running her fingers over the velvety smooth faux fur didn't compare. The friendly rabbit that allowed Nina to pet her had real fur or at least it felt much more real. Nina had never actually touched a real bunny before. Suddenly she had a brilliant idea, she had named her toy Nibbles so she decided to call the piano bunny the same name. One was a toy and the other was alive, or so it seemed.

When Nina's imagination gave way to slumber it picked up where it left off. Nina was running around inside the piano painting with

Nibbles while other bunnies hopped after them. Her giggles increased as she fell to the ground allowing Nibbles to hop up on her belly. Petting the little brown rabbit filled Nina with such merriment she never wanted to leave. As Nibbles fell asleep atop Nina she began to doze herself. Nina wasn't sure how long she'd been napping when she felt a cold breeze blowing on her face. Shivering from the chilly wind she opened her eyes. With a gasp, she found herself lying in tall green grass next to a dirt road in front of a towering house. There was a switchback staircase leading up to a spacious porch high above the ground. The front door of the barn style home appeared to be on the second floor. Nina would later learn there were cow pens on the ground floor beneath the house.

Something pulled at Nina and she soon found herself walking up the steps of the house onto the porch. The sound of mooing cows reached her ears, urging her to leave the porch and search out the source. Running around to the side of the expansive house revealed corrals filled with cows. Nina spotted numerous calves with their moms. Some were resting on the ground; others were nursing and many were jumping and leaping for the fun of it.

That's when Nina noticed the lush green rolling hills surrounding the house and corrals. Off in the distance she could see several more cows lazily grazing on the grass. The blue sky above was filled with the largest and whitest clouds she had ever seen. For some unknown reason the sky appeared bigger than ever before. It seemed like there was no end to it. Nina was staring at a cloud that resembled a jagged silhouette of a rabbit when the sound of horses broke her focus. Spinning around she spotted a wagon coming up the dirt road. Feeling no fear Nina waited anxiously for the wagon to reach the house. There was a wagoner urging the horses on, but what really caught Nina's attention was a young girl sitting next to the man driving the wagon. The girl appeared around Nina's age filling her with excitement. Having a friend in this wonderfully charming place could only make it extra fun.

The more the horses hurried towards the house the further the wagon appeared to be. The whole thing was nonsensical. Nina began running down the dirt road towards the wagon. Running faster than she ever had only increased the distance between her and the young girl. By now the young girl was standing on the seat holding tight to the wagoner's hand. Nina waved back and it was at that precise moment that Nina opened her eyes to find herself alone in her bedroom.

Heartbroken that her wonderful dream had ended was short lived. The sweet melodious sound of a music box reached Nina's ears. She didn't recognize the song and yet it sounded so familiar to her. Rushing from her bed she soon realized the sound was coming from her parent's room. Their door was open but neither of them were there. To make sure she whispered, "Mom? Dad?" No one answered so she ventured into their room. Climbing onto her parents bed she stood in amazement as Gram's music box played a soothing, fun and almost magical song. Nina couldn't help but smile as the song played on.

"Nina, what are you doing?" asked her dad from behind her.

"Listening to Gram's music box," replied an elated Nina.

Her dad walked closer, leaned close to the music box and said, "I don't hear anything."

The sweet-sounding song was gone. With exasperation and sorrow Nina collapsed on the bed. Looking up at her dad she muttered, "I heard it Dad. It was such a pretty song."

Marc wrapped his discouraged daughter in his arms then kissed her cheek. Not knowing the music box had been broken for years he said something that made Nina smile with anticipation, "Let me wind it back up for you angel."

Marc began winding up the music box making Nina giggle at the cranking sound. Once it was fully wound the music came back louder and clearer than before. Nina's beaming smile encouraged him to pick her up and start spinning in circles. He danced with his daughter until the song slowed then stopped with one final note. Nina threw her arms around her father's neck and squeezed tight.

"I have the album from the theatrical play this song is in. Would you like to hear it?"

"Is it as pretty as the music box?" Nina questioned.

"Nina. Nina it's time to get up." It was her mom's voice. Nina rolled over to see her mom standing in the doorway, "Come on sleepy head it's time to get up," coaxed Valerie sneaking towards Nina with a playful smile. Tickling her daughter until they were both laughing helped Nina momentarily forget that she had only dreamt the music box was working.

It was errand running day, so Valerie and Nina were out of the house early. Nina helped put the crackers, cookies and chips in the pantry before asking for an apple with crunchy peanut butter. Valerie put the rest of the groceries away while Nina watched TV from the dining table and finished her snack. A favorite animated movie kept Nina entertained while her mom cut the tags off Nina's new clothes and put them in the laundry. The busy day helped Nina forget about her dream and the song from Gram's music box.

Marc walked in the house with a bouquet of bluebells, red roses and carnations. He placed his index finger over his lips asking Nina to remain quiet. Having already removed his shoes he snuck up on his wife and wrapped his arms around her with the bouquet front and center for Valerie to see. She put the wooden spoon on the counter before spinning around inside his arms and placed a loving kiss on his lips. Nina being a normal nine-year-old squinched her face and covered her eyes. Even though she knew she was lucky to have parents that loved each other so much, she didn't want to see them kiss. There were far too many kids at her school whose parents were always fighting or divorced. Remembering this Nina soon uncovered her eyes and smiled as her parents embraced.

"You remembered," exclaimed Valerie talking a closer look at the bouquet which had become a tradition.

Marc lifted Valerie's face to his, tenderly kissed her lips and devotedly replied, "How could I ever forget the night I proposed to the love of my life?"

Valerie's face flushed, then she moved away from the stove revealing another tradition for the day. Lifting the lid of the Dutch oven released the savory aroma of mushrooms and short ribs. Valerie had been working on the meal from the moment they got home. It was completely a labor of love. Marc rushed to the refrigerator to find the Caesar salad and chocolate tart chilling inside. That's when he picked up on the scent of baby golden potatoes grilling in the oven making his stomach growl.

"Nina go wash up for dinner please," Valerie requested.

Nina's tummy had been growling for a while now, so she made quick work of washing her hands. Valerie had already served Nina her food, but she waited impatiently for her mom and dad to take their seats. Once everyone was seated the feast began. Nina had been looking forward to this special dinner ever since her mom told her what she was making. She gobbled down her food like she hadn't eaten a single thing the entire day.

Valerie decided long ago, when Nina had a mouthful of teeth, to cut tiny pieces of this special meal for her young daughter to enjoy. Nina loved it from the first taste. She was especially thrilled when she could eat the meat from the ribs. Eating such an adult meal at an early age made it seem no different to Nina than chicken nuggets or macaroni and cheese.

No matter how much Nina or her dad enjoyed their succulent dinner it was the chocolate tart that was their favorite. Almost in unison they used their forks to lift the first bite of the decadent dessert. As was their custom they stopped before putting the tart in their mouth and ever so carefully clanked their forks like a toast. Moving in slow motion they each put the bite in their mouths, closed their eyes and murmured yum. Valerie loved the fact that they had created their own tradition on this very special day.

Marc excused himself after helping clear the table. Nina wondered where he had gone as she finished her fruit punch. At first the sound of music was almost too soft to notice, but the volume got louder. Valerie put the plate she was holding in the sink, turned around and walked over to Marc who held out his arm for her.

"May I have this dance pretty lady?"

Reaching her husband Valerie placed her tiny hand in his saying, "Of course mi amor."

Watching her parents spin around the kitchen into the family room had Nina twirling on her own. As the two of them continued dancing around the house Nina found herself frozen in place. Both of her parents were so enthralled in their celebrating that neither of them noticed the look on Nina's face.

Soon Nina was shouting over the music, "That's the music box song!" She kept repeating herself until she finally got her mother's attention.

"Mi amor could you turn the music down?"

Marc walked over and turned the volume down until they could hear what Nina was so enthusiastically saying. A look of shock and amazement engulfed Valerie's face when she realized what Nina was shouting.

"What is it?" questioned a puzzled Marc.

Kneeling in front of her daughter Valerie calmly asked, "What did you say Nina?"

"That song is the song from Gram's piano music box," stated Nina as if there was nothing out of the ordinary.

Marc simply said, "See my pretty lady we were meant to be if that's the song from your grandma's music box."

"No, you don't understand," replied Valerie in a shaky voice. "The music box has been broken for years," Valerie returned her focus to Nina while Marc looked on with an expression of intrigue.

"Nina how do you know that was the song Gram's music box once played?"

Last night's dream came crashing back. Nina's mind raced through every moment of the dream in a matter of seconds. "I heard it in my dream last night. It was playing from the music box and when it stopped Dad wound it back up for me."

Wanting clarification Nina's dad asked, "If it's broken how could it play the song?"

"I don't know but that's what happened in my dream," stressed Nina.

Not wanting to upset Nina more than she already was, Valerie did her best to gloss over the entire subject, "Well that must have been a wonderful dream. I wish I had such wonderful dreams."

"It was Mama," Nina agreed, but she wasn't feeling any better about the situation. She recognized the song, she could even hum along to it, but how was the question.

Not another word was said all evening about the mystery of how Nina knew the song from her great-grandma's music box. Valerie refused to let all the questions running through her head take center stage over their special day. It was impossible for Nina to know what song the broken music box played, but somehow she did. Valerie repeatedly told herself there had to be a logical explanation and left it as that.

A Time to Dance

Nina's eyes popped open. She felt like something was wrong. She ran to her parent's room and found the bed made, her dad's briefcase was gone and she heard her mom milling around downstairs. Relief washed over her. She couldn't remember any dreams from the night before, but something had startled her awake. Nina climbed up on her parent's bed and with eagerness she looked for the piano, except there was a huge problem. Her great-grandma's music box wasn't there.

"Mom, Mom!" screamed Nina running to the top of the stairs.

The tone in Nina's voice made her mom stop what she was doing and rush to the stairs. "What's wrong?" she asked coming up the steps.

"Gram's music box is gone!" Nina answered with a cracking voice.

Valerie wiped the tears from Nina's eyes as she said, "Dad took it to a repair shop to see if they can fix it bumblebee."

It took a moment for Nina to feel better, but her mom's use of the nickname bumblebee helped. It was Valerie's own term of endearment for Nina. She came up with it in the hospital after receiving a very special one-of-a-kind gift from Theresa. It was the one and only handmade present Valerie received for her newborn daughter. Nina finally expressed her fear, "I thought someone had stolen it."

Not wanting to make her little girl feel worse Valerie hid her smile then reassured her, "No it wasn't stolen. Dad has it." Guiding Nina back to her room Valerie asked her to get dressed.

"Do you think it'll be fixed?" Nina's voice now was filled with excited anticipation. So much so she was jumping up and down on her bed.

"I don't know, but I'm hoping it will. Now stop jumping on the bed and get ready for the day. Breakfast is almost ready."

Summer break was one of Valerie and Nina's favorite time of the year. No homework or getting up early, instead their days were filled with fun. Coloring, treasure hunts, playdates, visiting

Grandma and so much more. Today however, Nina struggled to remain focused on their fun. Her mind kept wandering back to the possibility of the piano being fixed. When her dad returned from work she rushed into his arms, gave him his usual big squeeze and kiss on his cheek before blurting out, "Is the music box fixed?"

"Well at least you said hello before asking," he joked. "No angel it's not ready for me to pick up. The repairman said it won't be ready for a few weeks. He's a very busy man."

Nina's heart sank. To her a few weeks felt like a lifetime. Trying her best to remind herself that having it fixed was worth the wait she forced an unconvincing smile and said, "I guess a few weeks isn't that long."

"Just think bumblebee how happy you'll be if the repairman can fix it," Valerie interjected.

That did it. Nina couldn't wait to hear the song from the album last night coming from the piano music box. She had already decided the man was going to fix it. There was no doubt in her mind. Nina had ignored the use of the word "if" in her mom's sentence. The repairman would fix the piano; she just knew it.

For the next few days Nina had her mom play the album with the music box song on it. The album was old, but her dad's turntable was new, even though it had an old style look to it. Valerie was concerned the repairman wouldn't be able to fix the music box like so many before him. She knew Nina would be crushed. Valerie could sense her daughter had made up her mind about the piano being as good as new. Nina had been working on a dance that went with the song, confident that when the music box came home she could wind it up and dance along to it.

"Mom what is this song from?"

Valerie's face lit up with joyous remembrance. "It's from the play your father took me to the night he proposed to me."

"What's a play?"

"It's similar to a movie, except the actors are on a stage performing right in front of you. There's no screen like the TV. Imagine your favorite cartoon coming out of the television and being there right in front of you."

"That sounds like fun. Can we go see a play someday?"

"Yes we can, I'm sure we can find one you would like."

Nina asked with a turn of her head, "I wouldn't like the play you and Dad saw?"

"You're a little young for that one. You would probably be bored like you are when I watch my cooking shows," answered Valerie playfully hugging Nina. "Oh, that reminds me your name was almost Carmen because of that play."

"Instead of Nina?" asked Nina who shook her head saying, "I don't like the name Carmen. Nina is so much better."

"Well then we made the right choice."

"Ring, ring!" went the telephone.

Valerie picked up the phone and said, "Hello." Then she listened for a long time before saying anything. When she did, her words made Nina jump up and down. "My husband is working but I can swing by and pick it up. Thank you so very much for fixing the music box. Our daughter will," she looked over and saw Nina's merriment and edited her sentence midway through, "Our daughter is so excited."

Without being told Nina put her shoes on and stood by the door leading into the garage. As far as she was concerned her mom was taking much too long to get ready. At last they were on their way to the repair shop. Valerie pulled into a small shopping center. In her search to find which store had the music box Nina looked at all the window displays. There was a small pet store with kittens in the front window, which at any other time would have meant something to her, but Nina was on a mission.

When Valerie parked in front of a store with clocks and colorful figurines Nina was sure her mom was at the wrong place. Going inside didn't change Nina's mind. The walls were covered with all types of clocks, there wasn't room to mount one more. There were rows of display cases filled with everything from jewelry, watches, picture frames, jewelry boxes and snow globes. There wasn't a music box in sight, until Valerie walked up to the checkout counter. On either side of the cash register were display cases filled with music boxes of all shapes and sizes. Miniature carousals with horses, lots of rectangle ones, some made from wood, others were ceramic and ornately painted on all sides. It was a circular white base with a tiny bird cage spinning in a circle over red velvet that caught Nina's attention.

"That's a pretty one," said the man behind the counter.

Without even looking up Nina replied, "It is, but not as pretty as my great-grandma's piano music box."

With a big grin the plump elderly man agreed, "You are right about that. Let me go get your music box for you." Clearly Nina's comment had answered the man's unasked question of "Can I help you?"

The gentleman returned with a box held securely in his hands. Sitting the plain cardboard box on the counter he reached in and began unwrapping its contents from layers of bubble wrap. Finally, Gram's music box was revealed. He carefully turned the music box over and wound it up, just like Dad had done in Nina's dream. As the music started to play, Valerie's eyes welled up with tears and she covered her gasping mouth with her hand.

Nina immediately started to dance the dance she'd been working on. Valerie asked her to stop dancing to prevent her from bumping into something. That's when Nina noticed her mom's teary eyes. "What's wrong Mama?"

"I'm just so happy bumblebee. These are tears of joy," she reassured her daughter. Turning back to the repairman she had to ask, "How did you fix it? I mean it's been broken for so long and no one until now has been able to get it to work."

Proudly the man went on to explain about mechanisms being jammed. Years of dust, too much spring tension and other issues that Valerie didn't completely understand. It was all music box jargon which was something she knew very little about. He finished his rather lengthy description of all he had done by saying, "I'm just happy I could repair it for you. It clearly means a lot to you and your daughter. I must say though, I'm surprised no one was able to fix it prior to me. It wasn't that complicated to figure out."

With a shrug Valerie said, "I'm not sure, but all that matters to me is it now works."

After the music box was carefully repackaged it was paid for and put into a white bag. Valerie took hold of the twisted craft paper handles, thanked the man repeatedly and went to the car. Once they were on their way she told Nina they were going to stop by Grandma's condo to tell her the wonderful news.

Theresa opened the door saying, "What a nice surprise," upon seeing Valerie and Nina.

"We have an even better surprise," blurted Nina.

"Really? What is a better surprise than seeing you two?"

Nina giggled and spun in circles as she went inside the house. Valerie pulled the bag from behind her back and asked her mom to have a seat. Nina squirmed about as she impatiently waited for her mom to open the cardboard box and unwrap the surprise. Her annoyance grew as Valerie carefully and with deliberate movements unwrapped the music box, but once it was revealed she stopped wiggling about and looked at her grandma.

Trying not to be rude Theresa questioned, "My mom's music box is the surprise?" Then she wondered, "Are you returning it?"

With a panicked expression Nina looked at her mom. Silently hoping her mom would say no, but instead Valerie said, "Well that's up to you, but that's not the reason I brought it here." Valerie laid the piano upside down on her lap and carefully turned the music box winding key, making sure not to overwind it. When the music started playing Theresa burst into tears.

"Oh my gosh, it's working. How, when, who?" she blurted wiping the tears from her cheeks.

"Marc took it to the shop where he bought me my beautiful jewelry box. The repairman said it was going to take weeks before he'd have it ready, but it's only been a few days. When I picked it up the repairman was surprised it hadn't been fixed before. He said it wasn't too complicated to figure out what was wrong," explained Valerie.

Astonishment still covered Theresa's face. "That's amazing. I'm not sure why no one else could fix it. I had given up hope of ever hearing it play again. I guess this repairman is much better at his job than the others."

"I don't know. All I know is, it is working after all this time," Valerie paused and glanced over at her daughter. She then asked the question Nina didn't want to hear, "Mom, would you like to keep it until Nina is ten?"

Fighting back tears Nina placed her hands over her face leaving only her eyes and forehead visible. Grandma smiled at Nina then Valerie, knowing her granddaughter was trying to be brave. Theresa lifted the piano into her hands as the music slowed then stopped. She looked it over with love in her eyes. Appearing to be reminiscing made it impossible not to feel moved by her expressions. After what seemed like an eternity to Nina her grandma turned towards her and whispered in a shaky voice, "I'm beside myself with happiness having my mom's music box working after all these years, but I gave this to you Valerie to keep safe until Nina is ten. It should stay with you until then."

"As long as you're sure," confirmed Valerie.

Nina's face betrayed her trying to be a good girl and not make her grandma sadder. The desire to take the music box home over leaving it with Grandma was clearly evident. Thankfully Nina's following expression of pure joy and blissfulness upon hearing her grandma say she was sure made everyone smile.

"You can come visit the piano anytime you want," declared Nina throwing her arms around her grandma's neck.

Theresa squeezed her granddaughter and whispered in her ear, "Thank you jellybean, but you're the best part of my visits. Besides, I know the music box is in a safe place and you'll be ten before we know it."

Something is Coming

By the time Marc arrived home Valerie had to admit, at least to herself, that she was growing weary of listening to the music box play. Nina couldn't seem to get enough of it, but too much of even a good thing could become a bad thing. Valerie didn't want to wish for a second that the repairman hadn't fixed the little piano, but she wanted a break.

Nina showed off her dance a couple times for her dad, then he stepped in saying, "Nina you did a wonderful job making up that dance and I'm so happy you're happy, but how about we take a break from the music box and enjoy a quiet dinner."

Valerie's face said it all. Quiet filled the house except for the sound of silverware hitting the plates as the food was scooped up. Nina hadn't realized how hungry she'd gotten after dancing the day away. Her parents enjoyed an adult conversation, basically Marc's work, chores for the weekend and plans for an upcoming vacation.

The latter was the only one Nina listened to with interest. Without realizing it Nina had begun humming the tune from the music box. It wasn't until her dad pointed it out did she become aware of it and stop.

"I think Nina may have inherited my mom's singing ability," Marc expressed with a feeling of pride and heartache. He lost his mother a few years before Valerie knew she was pregnant. How he wished she had lived long enough to know a grandchild was on its way. Even more than that he wished Nina could have grown up with two grandmas in her life.

"Your mom could sing?" asked Nina.

"Your Grandma Candace had a beautiful singing voice. Your humming reminded me of a lullaby she would hum to me when I was little."

"Was it Gram's piano song?"

"No angel it wasn't, but your humming brought back memories of being lulled to sleep by my mom."

"What was the song?" Nina questioned, excited to hear more about the grandma she never knew.

Marc thought for a moment, then with a shake of his head admitted, "I don't remember the name."

Valerie teased, "Well if Nina can sing she didn't get it from either one of us."

"So true," agreed Marc, "I sing like my dad. He would try so hard to sing along with my mom. She would lovingly smile at him for trying, but I think it hurt her ears as much as mine."

After her bath Nina kissed her dad goodnight and climbed into freshly washed sheets. The lavender scent enveloped her making her suddenly feel very tired. Valerie read a short story to her sleepy daughter and as expected wrapped Nina in a big hug and kissed her cheek before saying "A squeeze and a kiss to take with you to dreamland."

Inaudible sounds escaped Nina's mouth, but Valerie knew she was trying to say, "Always Mama," as she drifted off to sleep. Closing the door gently Valerie went downstairs to find Marc asleep on the couch. Not at all ready for bed herself Valerie let Marc sleep as she pulled a photo album from the bookcase. It was a mishmash collection of random photo's. The first page had pictures of a camping trip she and Marc had gone on while dating. The next page held black and white pictures of Marc's mom and her family. Valerie smiled at a picture of Marc as an infant in his mom's arms surrounded by family members she couldn't quite recall. Adjacent to that page were newborn photos of Nina. Valerie believed Marc had deliberately placed his mom's pictures next to the first photos of Nina since she passed long before her granddaughter's birth.

As Valerie flipped the pages of the photo album memories came flooding back. There was only one 8 X10 picture in the entire album. It was a black and white professional photo of Valerie's grandma. Her long graying hair was pulled into a bun on top of her head and her closed mouth smile brightened up her attractive face. As Valerie soaked in the details of the picture she was unknowingly being watched by Marc.

In a hushed voice he asked, "What has you smiling?"

Valerie looked up at her husband with love radiating from her eyes. She turned the photo album page to him and answered, "My Grandma."

"You still miss her very much," commented Marc as he walked over to his wife. It wasn't a question; it was a statement. Valerie missed her grandma like Marc missed his mother.

"I do."

With a kiss on her cheek Marc suggested they go to bed. He had work in the morning and knowing Valerie like he did, she would stay up for hours looking through all the photo albums they had collected over the years.

At last the entire household was sound asleep. A cool summer's night breeze flowed through the master bedroom window making Valerie pull the sheet on top of her. The stillness of their home was interrupted every once in a while, by the icemaker dropping frozen crescents into the collection bin. The serenity of the house was in stark contrast to what was going on in Nina's dreams.

Out of the corner of her eye Nina could see things moving, but every time she turned her head to see what was around her it was too late. The sound of dogs barking, cats meowing and birds chirping made her believe there were animals surrounding her. Soon she could also hear horses and cows, but they too were darting around so fast she couldn't catch sight of them. Spinning around she did her best to surprise an animal to look at it, repeatedly failing. Nina wasn't afraid of animals, quite the contrary, she loved all animals. Which kept her somewhat calm. The sun was shining brightly and the smell of freshly cut grass made what was happening in the dream less frightening. However, the longer Nina found herself unable to catch sight of anything around her the more uncomfortable she became.

With a thud Nina hit the ground snapping her back to reality. Lying on the floor next to her bed she realized she had fallen out of bed. Her dad and mom rushed in wondering what the noise had been. Nina hadn't ever fallen out of bed before so the thump they heard was completely unfamiliar.

"Are you okay angel?" Marc asked rushing to pick up his daughter.

Feeling groggy from the heavy sleep she had been jerked from left her unsure what was going on. With a nod, she affirmed she was alright. Marc placed her back in her bed while Valerie pulled the sheet onto her saying, "Well that's the first-time that's ever happened."

"Where you having a nightmare?" asked her dad.

With a croaky voice she replied, "Not a nightmare, but I was spinning in my dream."

"Well you spun yourself right out of bed," stated Valerie.

With a yawn Nina replied, "I was trying to see the animals."

Valerie patted Marc on the back encouraging him to get some more rest before his alarm went off. Returning her focus on Nina she encouraged her daughter to go back to sleep without discussing the dream any further. She didn't want Nina to pick up where the dream left off and risk another fall out of bed. Nina being tired from her full day of dancing drifted off to sleep without a problem.

Nina noticed a bruise was forming on her elbow when she woke up. When she showed it to her mom Valerie came to the conclusion that it must have been from falling out of bed. During breakfast Nina did her best to try and explain the strange dream to her mom. The more Nina tried to explain the darting animals the less she understood the dream. Why would all the animals hide from her? Nina was confused by the animal's behavior. Not only did Nina love animals, animals loved her back.

"Thankfully it was just a dream bumblebee," Valerie reminded her.

Nina had completely forgot today was the day she had a playdate with Tiffany. Nina was ready in no time and so excited to tell Tiffany about the music box being fixed. After dropping Nina off Valerie finished up a few other chores before snuggling up on the couch to start a new book. The tranquility in her silent house was a welcome retreat from the commotion of the previous day. Thankfully Valerie had set a timer on the stove to remind her when to pick up Nina. She was almost halfway through her book when the alarm buzzed.

Nina hardly waited to get through the door of their house before asking to listen to Gram's music box. Valerie wished she had taken the music box back upstairs, out of sight out of mind, but she knew that probably wouldn't have helped. Hearing that song for the remainder of the day was a bit more than Valerie could handle. Besides she wanted to finish the chapter she was reading when the timer went off so she offered up a surprising suggestion, "Nina how about I wind it up and you can listen to it upstairs in your room?"

Nina's shocked expression was beat out by a huge smile, "Really mom? You'll put it in my room?"

Nina ran upstairs making herself stumble halfway up. Laughing she admitted, "I better slow down."

Valerie agreed as she carefully carried the music box into Nina's room. She placed the piano on the highest wall shelf after removing several stuffed animals. The music box was safely out of Nina's reach. I'm going back downstairs for a while to read, so when the music stops you're going to have to play for a bit until I come back upstairs.

Nina wasn't going to quarrel about the offer. She knew better than to question her mom on this. Any squabbling on her part would most assuredly end with Valerie taking the music box into her room and not letting Nina listen to the beautiful tune. Being a wise girl she said, "Okay Mom I'll wait for you to come back."

"That means no trying to touch the piano or trying to wind it yourself," warned Valerie.

"Got it."

After thoroughly winding the music box Valerie shut Nina's bedroom door and headed downstairs. Nina was captivated by the sight of the music box in her room. In an almost hypnotic stare she began humming along with the melody. Before she knew it, she was performing the dance she had choreographed. Closing her eyes for a mere moment changed everything.

Nina was on a theater stage complete with a red velvet curtain high above her showcasing the landscape scene behind her. The stage lights were zeroed in on Nina with a crowd of smiling people swaying along in their seats to the music box song. Without skipping a beat Nina completed her dance to a standing ovation and roaring applause. She took a bow and watched long stem red roses being thrown on stage from those in the front row. Next a well-dressed man with a top hat brought her a bouquet of red carnations tied together with a matching red ribbon.

Nina buried her nose into the sweet-smelling flowers and breathed deeply. Watching the crowd file out of the theater with bright happy faces made Nina chuckle. That's when she noticed a young girl waving at her from behind the last row of seats. It was too dark in the shadows and much too far away from the stage for Nina to make out any details about the girl. Yet somehow Nina knew it was the same girl who was riding in the wagon when she dreamt about the ranch house.

Nina climbed down off the stage and ran towards the back of the theater. The young girl did the same but before they could get close to each other the music box started to slow down eventually stopping and Nina was back in her room. Not wanting to forget her vision she took out her construction paper and crayons and went to work. She drew and colored faster than she ever had before. Her artwork had captured all she could remember. The background scene of rolling green hills with scattered cows grazing on them to the rows of red velvet seats and the large wooden doors beyond them. The theater was empty except for two people, Nina and the mysterious waving girl. Nina had done a remarkable job of blurring out the girl making her look fuzzy and void of too much detail.

Valerie was amazed at how involved Nina was in her coloring and surprised she didn't ask her to rewind the music box when she returned. Leaning over her daughter she commented, "That's a wonderful drawing bumblebee. Is it a theater?"

"Yes," Nina answered continuing to color in the roses on the stage.

"There's so much detail," exclaimed Valerie upon a closer look. "Did you see this in a movie or cartoon?" Before Nina could answer she asked one more question, "Who's that girl in the back?"

Nina raised her sorrowful face and her voice mirrored her heartache, "I don't know Mama...." Nina cut her sentence short. Something begged her not to finish what she was saying. Something deep inside her body and mind wouldn't let her complete her thought.

Nina's expression, tone and use of the word mama made Valerie wonder if Nina's dream from the night before was the cause. To make her daughter feel better she wound up the piano before asking Nina to dance for her. Nina did so, not only because her mom asked, but in hopes she'd see the little girl again. When the music faded away Valerie cheered like the crowd from the theater, bringing back Nina's beautiful smile.

Curiosity Grows

With such a busy and fun weekend, Nina found herself preoccupied with summer activities. Both Valerie and Marc made sure they didn't speak of great-grandma's music box as the two of them had grown exhausted from being asked to wind it up.

Nina ran up to her parents who were sitting on a park bench in the shade of a large sycamore tree. She grabbed a bottle of water and gulped down half of it before wiping her mouth with her arm and saying, "I was thirsty."

"I can tell," remarked her dad.

Valerie asked, "Would you like some more watermelon?"

Nina shook her head no and turned to leave, but her father's face and firm tone when he suggested that she stay in the shade and cool down a bit immediately changed her mind. She wouldn't admit it, but after having some watermelon under the shelter of the beautiful tree she did feel much better. Dad had been right, she needed to get out of the hot sun and cool down. Stepping out of the shade Nina enjoyed another piece of watermelon. Her eyes were drawn to the sky. She watched the few clouds above her shift from one shape to another as her parents continued their conversation. High above in the pale blue sky Nina noticed a black dot circling directly overhead. It didn't take long for her to realize it was a raven as the dot grew bigger in its descent.

"Hello Sable!" hollered Nina into the sky.

Her shout caught her parent's attention. Valerie questioned her daughter who Sable was. Nina was more than willing to finish telling her mom and dad about her dream at Gram's house. She told them everything from jumping off the swing to playing with Tiger and of course the shrinking in size. Valerie and Marc both thought her description of how Sable and Sunnee helped save them was quite interesting. The vivid details thoroughly impressed her parents.

With a smile of remembrance Valerie sighed, "I remember having an imagination like yours. Well, not quite as creative. Your imagination is much more like my grandma's, your great-grandma. How I wish you could have met her. She would have loved you so very much and being two peas in a pod I can't imagine the adventures you two would have gone on. There would have been no end to the inventive and clever stories your combined imaginations would have come up with."

Valerie unintentionally reminded Nina about Gram's music box. Even a couple more hours of play in the park didn't put a damper on Nina's excitement to listen to the music box when they returned home, but truth be told Valerie was happy to see Nina connecting with the great-grandma she never knew. If the heirloom piano and Nina's imagination somehow brought her closer to feeling like she knew her great-grandma so be it.

Marc came back downstairs after winding up the piano for Nina and said, "Boy that's some imagination Nina has. Those were amazingly specific details of your grandmother's house,"

Marc paused and asked, "Were any of them in her dream close to the truth?"

Valerie contemplated his question. Her eyes widen as she searched her memories. "Oh my gosh," replied an amazed Valerie, "A lot of the details were spot on. There was a large apricot tree in Grandma's back yard and she did dry her clothes on a clothes line, but I don't remember a swing set."

"Well, Nina was looking at a picture of your grandma in her backyard when she first told us some of her dream," reminded Marc not thinking too much about the similarities.

"But there was also a neighbor who had a cat that fit the description Nina gave and if I remember correctly his name was Tiger," Valerie continued explaining her grandma did play the piano and chicken soup was a favorite of hers. Pacing the floor Valerie racked her brain trying to see if there were any other details that matched Nina's dream.

Interrupting Valerie's mumbling Marc calmly expressed his original thought, "Baby, I'm sure Nina saw a picture of your grandma's home and you and your mom probably talked about it. You know kids, they're listening even when we don't think they are."

Unconvincingly Valerie said, "I suppose you're right."

Marc squeezed his wife and placed a kiss on her cheek. "Of course I'm right. I mean she couldn't have actually visited her great-grandma, even in a dream."

Valerie couldn't help but laugh at herself, "You're right mi amor. I'm not sure what I was thinking."

Meanwhile, upstairs Nina laid on her bed listening to the piano. Feeling tired from playing in the summer heat all afternoon her eyes began to blink with each blink becoming longer than the one before. Soon her eyes remained closed.

Nina opened her eyes and found herself back at the ranch house. This time she was standing next to the front door. Quickly she turned around eagerly looking for the wagon with the young girl to be coming up the dirt road.

Turning left then right and back again was in vain. The road was empty for as far as Nina could see. Suddenly from behind she heard a small voice say, "She's not coming."

Nina turned around and spotted a small bird that reminded her of a sparrow except it had a reddish face and chest. The bird was also thinner than any sparrow she'd seen before. Politely she asked, "Who's not coming?"

"I'm not going to spoil the surprise," chirped the tiny bird.

"Surprise?" Nina asked with a beaming smile.

Suddenly from below Nina heard a squeaky high pitched voice, "Hello Nina."

Looking down Nina saw a small mouse next to her feet. She bent down to get a better look and discovered that the mouse looked very different from the ones at the pet store. The small rodent had elongated hind feet and a very long tail. Her deep black eyes stood out against the yellowish-orange fur on her sides and the dark brown band that ran down the center of her back. Standing up on her hind legs the mouse asked, "Would you extend your hand so I can climb up?"

Without any hesitation Nina knelt down and put her hand on the porch. She couldn't help but giggle as the nails of the mouse tickled her palm when it climbed aboard. Nina stood back up prompting the little bird to join the mouse on her hand. The two carried on a conversation for a moment, but due to them whispering Nina couldn't hear them. She leaned in and tried to listen to their tiny voices but to no avail. That's when the bird made an abrupt departure.

"What happened?" Nina questioned thinking she had frightened the bird off.

"I sent her on a mission," replied the mouse. "Allow me to introduce myself. I'm Kumah and I'll be your guide for today."

"Nice to meet you Kumah. Why do I need a guide?"

"You'll see," cheered the mouse jumping up and down in Nina's hand. "Follow me!" directed the mouse jumping onto the porch railing and making her way down into the front yard. Nina could hardly control her anticipation. Rushing down the stairs she skipped the two final steps and jumped onto the dirt walkway.

The little mouse was remarkably fast as she leapt towards the tall grass. Nina lost sight of her mere steps into the grasslands but she kept moving in the direction Kumah had headed. Nina stopped dead in her tracks when she noticed a large-eared buck on the horizon. The deer's far reaching rack made him an impressive sight. Nina admired his beauty, but also wondered if it were difficult for the buck to balance his expansive antlers. The sunlight made his reddish-brown coat shimmer. Without warning the large animal headed Nina's way and yet she felt no fear.

The deer slowed down then stopped still quite a distance from Nina, he bowed lowering his antlers close to the ground. After lifting his majestic head the stag bound towards her. He stopped just far enough away to repeat his bow directly in front of Nina. Standing upright he dwarfed her with his size. He was magnificent as he stood there tall and proud before introducing himself, "It's an honor to meet you Nina. I'm Tarak and I'll watch over you on your adventures." As he spoke he slowly closed the gap between himself and Nina.

Before Nina could ask Tarak why she needed to be watched over Kumah interrupted. "He's the best guardian we have. That's even what his name means," boasted Kumah who was clinging to one of his tines.

Tarak remained motionless in a regal stance. He waited for Nina to address him and she took his intent stare as a clear indication of such. "My apologies Tarak. It's nice and an honor," she added remembering his introduction, "to meet you."

Tarak's next words were a bit surprising, "What would you like to do first Nina?"

His unexpected question left her speechless. She wasn't sure where she was or what her options were. Then she remembered the girl, "I'd like to meet the girl I saw in the wagon and the theater."

"Today is not the day for introductions between you two. That will have to wait until the time is right," stated Tarak in a tone Nina knew not to question. She had been taught respect. Never in her wildest dreams did Nina imagine she would need to show respect to a talking deer, but here she was.

The more she was told she wasn't going meet the mysterious girl who kept waving at her, the more desperate Nina became to meet her. Why was it such a secret? If they weren't supposed to meet why did the girl keep showing up? Nina's mind raced with endless questions until Kumah interrupted her thoughts.

"It'll all make sense in time," Kumah reassured her, "But for now there's many more things we could do."

"Like what?" asked Nina hoping she'd get some answers.

Kumah leaped from one tine to another. After landing and before jumping to another she proposed a different idea. She suggested going down to the river, milking a cow, picking wildflowers and several more, but her last idea was the winner.

Nina announced her selection with great excitement, "I want to ride Tarak over the hills and see more of this beautiful place."

Tarak crouched down allowing Nina to climb on top of his massive back. He highly advised Nina to hold on tight. He moved slowly at first until he could feel Nina settle into the rhythmic movement of his ambling. Before long he quickened his pace until Nina leaned forward and took hold of the base of his antlers. He gradually moved from his leisurely stroll to a brisk walk then full steam ahead into jaunty strides. Nina laughed so hard she almost fell off forcing Tarak to halt.

That's when Nina took a good look at her surroundings. Pine trees dotted the bright green rolling hills encompassing them and just as it was the last time she visited the sky seemed endless. It appeared bluer, larger and so much more impressive than the sky at home. The sound of rushing water suddenly caught her attention and she asked, "Could we get a drink of water?"

"Of course Nina. Would you like to walk the rest of the way?" Tarak asked sounding a bit like he hoped her answer would be no.

She said she would like to walk and slid off Tarak landing hard on the ground. "That was a long way down," expressed Nina thankful the grassy field was a soft place to land.

"Are you injured?" a concerned Tarak asked.

"Nope, it was just a little further than I expected. Now which way to the water?"

"I'll show you the way."

Nina walked alongside Tarak while Kumah stayed on his antlers. Approaching a patch of trees Nina could tell they were close to their destination by the increased sound of the rushing water. Making their way through the trees Nina noticed the respect the other animals showed Tarak as he walked by. None of them spoke, but they all lowered their heads as he passed before them. Upon reaching the crystal-clear water Nina knelt down and scooped the cold refreshing liquid to her lips. Who knew water could taste so amazing. She drank her fill before standing up and asking, "Where's the water coming from?"

"There are two waterfalls a few miles away that both feed into this river," replied Tarak.

"Can we go see them?"

Before Tarak could answer Nina heard the blaring sound of fire truck sirens. She turned her head and saw her bedroom window. Frantically Nina rubbed her eyes hoping when she reopened them she would be back at the river, but she wasn't. The music box was still playing so she hadn't dozed off for long. Yet it felt like so much time had passed.

Nina hollered downstairs, "Is dinner almost ready?" She felt famished and barely noticed the music box abruptly stopped.

"No, but you can have a snack," suggested Valerie.

"When will dinner be ready?" questioned Nina walking into the kitchen.

Her mom looked at her with a look of bewilderment, "It's not even close to dinner time bumblebee."

How was that possible? Nina felt like she had been asleep for hours and she was so hungry. Where did the time go? It was at that moment Nina remembered the music box had suddenly stopped instead of fading off like it normally did. This worried Nina. She feared it was broken again and shared that with her mom in a frantic tone. There was no getting Nina to settle down and eat her snack without first checking the music box. They all headed up stairs. Carefully Marc wound up the piano and without fail it started playing. Nina didn't understand it, but all she cared about was it worked.

"See it's fine angel."

Nina felt better and said, "I'll have that snack now."

An Imaginary Day

It had been a bustling summer for Nina's family. Valerie checked the calendar and remarked, "Nina we need to start shopping for your new school clothes and supplies."

Nina enjoyed shopping for new clothes, but her favorite thing to shop for were all the school supplies. She would pick out the brightest folders, most colorful pencils and a pencil holder that was not only cute on the outside but had pockets, dividers and most importantly straps that held each pencil individually in place. Nina liked her things organized. She would spend hours organizing and reorganizing her pencil case until she found the perfect spot for everything.

Sadness repeatedly gripped Nina knowing school was only a few weeks away and she had yet to have another dream about the ranch or the girl she so desperately wanted to meet. She missed all her animal friends, but mostly she missed visiting Gram at her home. Nina had all but given up on having another magical dream, so much so that she agreed to put the piano back in her mom's room. This surprised both her parents, but Nina explained it away saying she wasn't ten yet and that was the agreement she had made with her grandma.

When the music box was moved into her parent's room Nina felt a sense of relief. Her frustration and growing despair about no longer having amazing dreams no matter how many times she listened to the music box was taking a toll on her bubbly personality. Something the entire family was beginning to notice, including Grandma, although they had no idea it was caused by the music box and lack of enchanting dreams.

Returning home from a successful shopping trip Valerie got busy with removing tags and washing Nina's new wardrobe. Meanwhile, upstairs in her room Nina began the relaxing and enjoyable task of organizing her pencil case. Dumping the pencils, erasers, scissors, gel pens, little notebooks and glue stick on her bed filled her with excitement. She tore open the packaging tossing it on the floor and began examining her options in the pencil case. That's when she heard the piano playing from her parent's room. She looked up and softly said, "Mom?" but there was no answer.

Nina walked to her bedroom door. Mom was nowhere in sight and after carefully listening she could hear her mom switching the laundry downstairs. That's when the volume of the music box reached a thunderous level. Nina started to head towards her parent's room, but something utterly shocking happened. "Nina where are you going?" squeaked a tiny voice from behind her.

Nina immediately spun around and with wide eyes spotted Kumah on her bed. The little mouse was struggling to hold a pencil in her hands which was teetering one way then the other until it landed on the bed. Kumah laughed the cutest laugh Nina had ever heard. Kumah giggled saying, "I did my best, but your pencils are just too long."

Nina rushed back into her room managing to take the time to quietly close her door. Kneeling down beside the bed Nina asked, "Kumah what are you doing here? How did you get...."

Cutting in Kumah smiled, ignored Nina's question and asked, "How can I help you with your school stuff?"

Taken back by the surprise visit and that she was wide awake Nina decided not to waste such an unbelievable moment. "First let's find a place for my scissors, then we can do all the pencils, pens and whatever is left."

The two chatted about the ranch, how Tarak was doing and how big the calves had grown. In no time the pencil case was done making Nina fearful that Kumah would disappear as quickly as she appeared. That wasn't the case. Nina and Kumah played a game of checkers which Nina lost, then they had a tea party and of course Nina showed Kumah the dance she had made up. The music box was still playing and it did so long enough for Nina to teach Kumah the dance. It was the most adorable thing Nina had ever seen and she laughed with her entire body as Kumah danced around the bed.

All that dancing and playing had made Nina hot so she opened her bedroom window revealing another surprise guest. Sunnee was holding on to the outside of the screen and asked to come in. Nina wasn't sure what to do. She couldn't cut the screen. Dad wouldn't like that one bit. She thought long and hard becoming so involved in her train of thoughts that she failed to notice Kumah had chewed a tiny slit in the screen just big enough for Sunnee to squeeze through.

Sunnee fluttered around in front of Nina's face until Nina lifted her hand allowing Sunnee to land on her index finger. "How'd you get in?"

"I let her in," answered Kumah proudly.

Upon further investigation Nina noticed the tiny slit in the screen. It wasn't terribly big, but she knew her dad would wonder how it got there. Feeling Sunnee flitter about on her finger brought her focus back to her visitors. Nina would worry about Dad discovering the tear in the screen later, right now she wanted nothing more than to have fun with her friends.

Sunnee flitted about the room in a dance all her own as Kumah and Nina performed the dance she had choreographed. Nina lost count as to how many times they completed the dance, eventually growing tired of it. Carefully sitting on her bed making sure Kumah was safely out of the way she asked, "What should we do next?"

Sunnee was quick to reply, "How about we go see your great-grandma. I haven't visited her in quite a while."

Before Nina could get a word out, they were standing in Gram's kitchen. Tiger was the first to notice the guests. He jumped from his chair and welcomed them, which got Gram's attention. Her face lit up when she saw them and said, "What a wonderful surprise."

Nina sank into her great-grandma's hug, closed her eyes and breathed in deeply the scent of Gram's sweater. It smelled like the wildflowers that grew in her backyard near the clothes line. Nina didn't know it, but even when she grew older the scent of wildflowers would forever remain one of her favorite smells. "It's so great to see you Gram. I've missed you."

"And I've missed you. I was beginning to think I wasn't going to see you again."

"I didn't know how to get back," replied Nina with grief in her voice. Her tone suddenly changed when she announced, "Sunnee helped me find my way back."

"Thank you Sunnee, that was very kind."

Sunnee flew over to Gram and landed on her shoulder. That's when Gram noticed Kumah and questioned, "Who do we have here?"

"I'm Kumah," answered the small creature who sprung towards Gram with long leaps. Gram put out her hand and welcomed the mouse into her home.

Nina was happier than she had ever been. She had wonderful extraordinary friends and most importantly she was once again with her Gram. She wondered to herself if the day could get any better and then it did. Nina helped Gram sort pinto beans at the kitchen table. Kumah quickly consumed the pile of discarded beans saying it was a waste to throw them out so she'd eat them instead. Looking across the table at Kumah feasting, Tiger sorting beans and Sunnee resting on the table top filled Nina with unknown joy. Of course, that's when it all ended.

"Nina here's your laundry to put away," declared Valerie breaking the special moment.

Startled by her mom's sudden appearance at Gram's house made Nina jump. She turned her face towards the sound of her mom's voice and to her dismay she was back in her room. She looked around the room and both Sunnee and Kumah were gone. Bewilderment didn't come close to expressing how Nina felt. Clearly the puzzlement Nina felt over what had just happened was evident on her face.

"Is something wrong?" Valerie asked.

Nina was speechless. Noticing her pencil case was packed just like she and Kumah had done and the checker board was still on the bed only added to her confusion. She wanted to see if her screen still had the slit in it but she didn't want to draw attention to the damage Kumah had done. The weight of her mom's stare broke through Nina's thoughts and she quickly responded, "No, nothing's wrong."

Valerie knew that tone. "What aren't you telling me?"

Nina knew the more she tried to convince her mom everything was fine the less Valerie was going to believe her. Most mom's just have a sixth sense when it comes to their children telling stories or lies. Knowing she couldn't explain her day, Nina decided to fess up about the slit in the screen. "When I opened my window I noticed a tear in the screen, but it's little," Nina added trying to downplay the situation.

Valerie walked over to examine the damage. "That's not too bad," she commented then upon a closer look she said, "It looks like it's been gnawed at." That was it. The jig was up. How could Nina explain that her friend Kumah, who happened to be a jumping mouse had visited? Nina was sure the cat was out of the bag, but then her mom said something surprising. "It looks like we have mice in the vines again." Valerie closed the window telling Nina to leave her window closed until her dad could repair the screen.

Nina breathed a sigh of relief when her mom left. Valerie didn't question Nina as to how the screen got damaged, she simply thought of a reason herself, keeping Nina from having to try and explain Kumah or worse lie to her mom. Standing silent in her room is when Nina noticed the music box was no longer playing and the sound of her dad returning home from work meant she had been in her room for hours.

"I'm home angel, where's my hug and kiss?" shouted her dad.

Nina ran downstairs and leaping from the third step she was caught in her father's arms. She kissed his cheek and squeezed with all her might. Marc laughed and pretended he couldn't breath as Nina tried to tighten her hug even more. They both knew she wasn't really cutting off his air supply, but it had become a fun tradition.

Valerie announced dinner would be ready in half an hour. Enough time for Marc to wash up and relax a bit while Nina headed back upstairs to put all her new clothes away. Standing on her bright yellow step stool Nina hung up her clothes reliving the day's events. From shopping with her mom to her guest's surprise visit and seeing Gram it had been a full day. They all seemed to blend together like a normal day, but the most extraordinary part of her day was anything but normal. She could easily explain away organizing her pencil case, but not the checkboard on her bed or the rip in her window screen. Upon placing the last pair of new shoes on her closet floor she couldn't help but wonder if she had fallen asleep while putting her things in the pencil box. That could be it she thought to herself but the slit in the screen seemed to be shouting at her, "It was real Nina, it was real!"

During dinner Marc discussed a new project he was working on as well as a new-hire he had big plans for. Her parent's conversation gave Nina time to contemplate the unusual events of her day. The more intently she thought about them the more the pain in her head intensified.

"Are you alright bumblebee?" asked Valerie noticing Nina was rubbing her head.

"I have a headache," Nina moaned.

"I hope you're not coming down sick."

"It's just my head, nothing else hurts."

Valerie got up from the table and walked over to the cabinet where the medication was, "I'll give you some medicine that should help."

Nina chewed and swallowed the two bubble-gum flavored tablets without complaint proving her head really did hurt. After finishing her meal Marc carried her up to bed and tucked her in with a gentle kiss on her forehead. "Feel better angel," expressed Marc hoping Nina would rest peacefully. By the time Valerie made it to her room Nina was already sleeping. Valerie placed the crocheted bumblebee her mom had made and brought to the hospital when Nina was born next to her. The treasured gift was showing signs of wear after nine years of play and a constant bedtime companion.

Nina woke up in the exact same position her dad had placed her in. She felt much better than the night before. Her headache was gone and she had decided to simply remember yesterday's events with child-like innocence and appreciation.

Maybe it was nothing more than her astonishing imagination playing games with her. Her mom and grandma kept telling her how inventive her playtime was after all. Remembering that her creativity mirrored her great-grandmas made her smile fondly.

That's when Nina heard voices and strange noises outside her bedroom window. She peered outside and saw a work truck parked in front of their house. On the side of the white truck were pictures of bugs on their back with red lines across them. Nina knew who was there, it was the exterminator that came to spray for bugs and although there wasn't a mouse on the truck Nina felt fearful. Nina rushed downstairs, "Why is the bug guy here?"

Nonchalantly Valerie replied, "He's checking to see if we have mice."

"What's he gonna do if we have mice?" Nina asked hoping the answer wasn't going to be what she was thinking.

"He'll get rid of them for us," Valerie replied without giving any specifics.

"He can't kill them!" shrieked Nina turning to run outside.

That's when Marc came inside reassuring Nina the exterminator didn't find any signs of mice. After verifying the truck had left Nina relaxed. Her parents were so excited they didn't have a mouse problem that the rip in Nina's screen turned into a minor issue. Valerie suggested she try to stitch the small tear together so Nina could open her window if she wanted without letting bugs in.

Wanting the entire thing to go away Nina said, "That takes care of that," a phrase Grandma Theresa uses all the time. Both Marc and Valerie chuckled at Nina mimicking her grandma, while all Nina could think about was that was way too close for comfort.

Sad News

All too soon it was the first day of school. Nina was happy about school starting. She enjoyed school and missed her friends, but there was a dark cloud hovering above her. Not once since Kumah and Sunnee's last visit had Nina traveled to see Gram or the ranch. No matter how many times she asked her parents to wind up the music box.

Valerie was thrilled to see the excitement on Nina's face when she picked her up from school. On the walk home Nina talked non-stop about who was in her class, how much she already liked her new teacher and the new playground equipment the school had put in over the summer. Nina gave her mom a stack of papers she needed to fill out when they got home. Nina didn't have any homework but her mom sure did. Enjoying this turn of events made Nina happy and she soon danced her way up the stairs leaving Valerie to complete her task.

No sooner did Nina reach the top of the stairs did she hear the music box song. She rushed into her parent's room and sure enough the piano was playing. Before she could wonder too much about why it was playing she heard from behind her, "How was school Nina?" Spinning around she spotted Tiger on her parent's bed. He rolled over and playfully stretched his front legs towards her coaxing her to pet him.

"What are you doing here?" questioned Nina as her affectionate petting prompted Tiger to purr loudly.

Too involved in enjoying the attention he was getting he didn't answer her, so Nina stopped petting him. He climbed up on her lap and nuzzled her hand trying to get her to start petting him again while saying, "Gram was wondering how your first day of school went."

Nina's heart skipped a beat, "Is Gram here?"

"No silly, but you can come see her."

"How?"

Tiger jumped from Nina's lap saying, "Follow me," as he ran into the hallway.

Nina followed him without hesitation although it didn't make any sense. When her second foot left her parent's room she found herself standing in Gram's kitchen. The smell of homemade taquitos frying in Gram's well-seasoned cast iron skillet engulfed Nina's senses. Nina ran to Gram throwing her arms around her waist. "I hope you're hungry," remarked Gram removing the last taquito from the pan.

"I am!" exclaimed Nina taking a seat at the table.

Gram told Nina to go wash up with a huge smile which made her eyes light up, one of Nina's favorite things about her Gram. It was as if the love in Gram's heart shone through her dark-chocolate brown eyes. Nina repeated all she had told her mom about school as they ate. They continued talking while they washed the dishes, put the few left-over taquito's in foil and refilled their glasses with lemonade. "How about some apricot crisp for dessert?"

Nina was in full agreement about the dessert although she wasn't entirely sure what apricot crisp was. She knew she liked apricots and loved desserts making her sure she would enjoy whatever it was. Gram grabbed a rectangle pan from the kitchen counter and asked Nina if she would get the whipped cream. Nina ran to the fridge and looked for the delicious topping. She searched high and low, but she couldn't find the aerosol can she knew was in her refrigerator at home.

"Gram I can't find it?" replied a disappointed Nina. Adding whipped cream to any dessert made it better. She was sad not to find any.

Gram reassured Nina it was in the refrigerator and told her what to look for, "It's in the white bowl with blue flowers on it."

Nina spotted a white glass bowl with blue flowers covered with plastic wrap. Using two hands she pulled it from the lowest shelf in the refrigerator and sure enough it was full of white fluffy stuff. "I've never seen it in a bowl before," commented Nina slowly making her way over to the table.

"I make my own," replied Gram cutting a piece of apricot crisp for Nina. "I use heavy cream, sugar and vanilla then I whip it myself. That turns it into whipped cream."

"I didn't know you could do that."

Gram scooped a large spoonful of the whipped cream onto her and Nina's dessert before saying, "Once you taste it you will see why I make it myself."

Gram was right. The whipped cream was so much better than the aerosol kind and it was the perfect addition to the apricot crisp. Nina used her fork to scrap her plate as clean as she could. Gram beamed with pleasure watching her great-granddaughter devour her dessert. "Should I take your empty plate as a sign that you like apricot crisp?"

"Yes, I liked it very much," Nina agreed licking her lips clean.

"What would you like to do next?" asked Gram.

Tiger who was stretched out on the kitchen floor soaking up the last bit of sunshine answered before Nina opened her mouth, "How about we go outside and chase birds?"

"I don't want to chase birds," opposed Nina thinking about Sable and the little reddish bird from the ranch.

"Okay, no bird chasing."

Nina shared what she was thinking, "I thought you liked Sable."

"I do, but it's fun to chase birds it's good exercise. I don't catch them Nina."

"Well that's good news, but I still don't think it's very nice," she said crossing her arms.

Gram started washing their plates and forks before suggesting she and Tiger go in the backyard, confident they would find something they'd both like to do. From the kitchen window, she watched Nina run full-steam ahead to the swing set while Tiger climbed high into the apricot tree.

Nina repeatedly swung higher and higher always jumping far into the grass. Each time she tried to go further than the time before. By the time Gram joined them outside Nina's face was beet red and darkness was swallowing up the backyard. That's when Nina noticed Gram had brought out a glass of lemonade. With a final leap from the swing Nina ran over and guzzled down the entire glass of lemonade. She used the back of her forearm to wipe her mouth dry which resulted in Gram saying the same thing her mom says, "Use a napkin please." Nina obliged.

Gram suggested they go inside as it was getting late. There was something different in Gram's expression and Nina wanted to know what was wrong. It almost looked like she was trying really hard not to cry.

"Why do you look sad Gram?" wondered Nina.

Tiger jumped up in Gram's lap while she took a moment to answer. Even Tiger looked unhappy and Nina knew something was terribly wrong when he didn't purr no matter how much Gram petted him. Raising her face to Nina she did her best to explain, but none of it made any sense.

"Nina my sweets, I can't tell you how much I've loved our visits. Seeing you is a dream come true and I will forever treasure our time together. You are very much like me as a child and knowing that makes me truly happy because it makes me feel like I'm living on in my amazing great-granddaughter."

Nina wondered why Gram was talking like she was about to say goodbye. Nina rushed into her Gram's arms and held on tight believing if she hugged her tight enough and long enough Gram wouldn't finish what she was saying. Nina needed to stop Gram before she said something she couldn't take back. Fighting against her welling eyes proved futile. The tears began streaming down Nina's face at the mere thought of what was coming. Nina remembered saying goodbye to a friend who moved away and this felt very much like that day. Her mind raced wondering why Gram would go away.

Gram released Nina, wiped away her tears and pulled her up onto her lap. Even in the dim light Nina could see a single tear roll down Gram's cheek and then she went on with what she was saying, "I know this isn't easy for either of us, but it's the way it has to be. There are some things you can't fight against, no matter how much you wish you could. Take gravity for instance. No matter how much you would love to float away, you can't. Gravity holds you to the ground no matter how hard you fight against it." Gram paused before stating, "This is the last time we can visit sweets. I can't see you after today."

Nina didn't care about gravity, she cared about her Gram and visiting her. Determined to fight she had a suggestion Nina hoped would be the answer they were looking for, "Can Mom, Dad and Grandma come here?"

"No, they can't. It doesn't work that way. Besides the magic no longer works for your mom or grandma."

"Then I'll stay here!" blurted Nina.

Gram appreciated the sentiment but knew better and said, "Oh no sweets, your parent's and grandma would miss you far too much." Clearly there wasn't any way for Gram to ease Nina's pain. She decided to treat it like removing a bandage by quickly ripping it off instead of slowly pulling it from one's skin. In hopes of lessening their pain Gram decided to get it done as quickly as possible. She lifted Nina's face to hers, kissed her cheek and said, "I love you very much Nina and I'm going to miss you more than I can say, but remember there's so much more waiting for you. You're going to go on wondrous magical adventures and meet lots of new friends." Gram embraced her great-granddaughter one more time before tearfully whispering, "Goodbye sweets," into Nina's ear.

Nina immediately looked up towards her Gram and found she was staring at the ceiling of her parent's room. The room was silent making Nina turn towards the piano as it slowed to a near stop. Tears rushed from Nina's eyes feeling heartbroken that she wouldn't see Gram again. That's when Tarak's voice resonated throughout the room, "Don't cry Nina. Your Gram spoke the truth, there is so much more waiting for you. Your magical adventures are just getting started. Be brave dear one and know we will see each other soon." Simultaneously, when Tarak spoke his last word the final note from the music box faded into silence.

"Nina," called her mom from the bottom of the stairs, "I have your paperwork done, come and get it."

As Nina walked downstairs she noticed the sun was shining brightly in the house. It had been nighttime at Gram's. Nina wondered how that was possible. "Thank you mom," muttered Nina still sad over leaving Gram. Without another word, she headed upstairs before Valerie could see the tears now racing down her face.

After hours passed Valerie called Nina down for dinner, but she was still full from eating at Gram's house. She washed her hands and face before heading down hoping her freshly washed face would hide the fact that she'd been crying. Valerie was so busy putting the finishing touches on dinner that she didn't even turn towards Nina when she came downstairs. Nina was still concerned her mom would ask her if she'd been crying and that was a conversation she didn't want to have. Nina had no idea how or what she'd tell her mom. She couldn't tell her the truth her mom wouldn't believe her. Valerie was sure to chalk it up to Nina's talented imagination and wonder why she was crying over her playtime.

Nina waited on the couch watching cartoons until she heard the garage door open signaling her dad was home from work. She ran into the downstairs bathroom and confirmed her flush face was gone. Thankfully she looked fine, but she still wasn't hungry. Nina forced down a couple bites then lazily played with her food which didn't go unnoticed by her mom.

"Aren't you hungry?" Valerie asked.

"Not really," Nina answered afraid if she talked too much she would start crying again.

"I still think you're coming down sick," Valerie declared placing her cheek against Nina's forehead to check for a fever. Lifting her daughter's face to hers she said, "Well your eyes look glassy, that's not a good sign."

What a wonderful turn of events. Between her sorrowful eyes looking glassy and her lack of appetite she had a way out of her predicament.

"Do you want to go to bed angel?" Marc asked.

"Yeah," was all Nina said.

Before heading up to bed Marc gave his daughter a hug and kiss saying, "I'm sure you'll feel better in the morning. You're probably tired from your first day back to school."

Nina was thankful both of her parents were finding their own reasons for her unusual behavior. Once ready for bed Nina and her mom shared their goodnight ritual leaving Nina laying wide awake in her bed. Reliving each and every visit she had with her Gram made her feel both happy and sad at the same time. She continued her trip down memory lane until she heard her mom and dad coming upstairs to go to sleep. She rolled over in bed putting her back to the door and laid deathly still when her mom checked on her.

Before long the house was eerily quiet and Nina found herself focusing on the tree outside her window, the branches were blowing in the night's gentle breeze. In an almost hypnotic rhythm the swaying tree branches lulled Nina to sleep. Come morning she felt a renewed hope and anticipation for the new adventures both Gram and Tarak had told her about. She still missed Gram and the mere thought of never seeing her again made Nina terribly upset and yet there was this newfound expectancy beating inside her chest. Each time her heart ached from missing Gram she heard Tarak's words echo inside her head. The sound of his voice soothed away the heartache replacing it with excitement over what was to come. This new unexplainable excitement was stronger than her need to cry over missing Gram, something Nina couldn't explain but wholeheartedly appreciated. By the time Valerie came in to check on Nina and see if she wanted to go to school Nina was already dressed.

"Feeling better I see," said Valerie happy to see Nina looking like herself.

"Yep, all better." Nina couldn't understand it. Tarak hadn't told her anything specific about what was coming. Yet somehow his reassuring tone was mysteriously wiping away the intense pain of saying goodbye to Gram.

An Incredible Journey

The school week went by quickly. Between being at school and homework Nina had little time to think about the music box and missing Gram. Things were getting back to what it was like before learning about great-grandma's piano. It wasn't until Saturday morning when her parents were already outside doing yard work did Nina have time to go into their room and look at the piano. After a few minutes Nina climbed off the bed to head downstairs to get some food. When her feet hit the floor, she heard the familiar sound of the music box being wound up. She couldn't reach the piano so she climbed back onto the bed and stood on her tippy toes. Nothing out of the ordinary was there. She bent over and watched as the wind key kept turning.

Nina no longer wondered how the music box would start playing on its own, but to watch it wind itself was a bit unnerving. She reminded herself that all that mattered was when it randomly started to play there was an adventure waiting for her. Nina waited for something to happen yet nothing changed. She was still standing in her parent's room when out of nowhere a memory came crashing back. The day Grandma had moved to her new place was the same day the piano was rediscovered in a carefully packed box. Grandma and Mom had shared a memory they'd both forgotten about, but what was it?

Nina racked her brain trying to recall what it was they shared. She clearly remembered the butterfly flying across the piano lid, how her great-grandma would wind it up for her grandma when she was a little girl and then it hit her. "Play me a tale!" pleaded Nina staring at the piano.

That's all it took. Nina was standing on the rolling hills behind the ranch where she first met Tarak. Much to her delight he was standing there too. He bowed his head causing his large rack of antlers to straddle Nina on either side and said, "Good job dear one. I knew you would figure out how to make the music box's gateway work."

Exhilaration pulsed through Nina's veins at the thought of visiting the ranch whenever she liked by simply reciting the phrase, "Play me a tale." Jumping up and down she asked, "So I can come here anytime I want?" Then she remembered, "Gateway?"

"Not anytime," Tarak answered, "We have to make sure your parents are busy and won't notice your disappearance."

"I disappeared?" questioned a concerned Nina who no longer cared about the gateway comment.

"Fear not dear one. The magic will let us know if your parents decide to look for you and you'll be whisked away before they realize you're no longer at home." Tarak gave his answer as if there wasn't anything the slightest bit unusual about it. Being transported between worlds was clearly a normal part of life here, but not where Nina was from. As she contemplated his reply he interrupted her thoughts by saying, "Your mom and dad will never know you're gone unless you seem unsettled when you're spontaneously sent home."

"Unsettled?" Nina understood the word easy enough, it had been a vocabulary word in last week's homework, but she knew she would have to work on not feeling troubled upon suddenly returning home. The memory of the last time she saw Gram and the difficulty she had hiding her emotions and teary eyes from her parents made her concerned.

Tarak reassured her that she would get used to traveling back and forth through the portal adding, "It will soon become second nature and your body will start to recognize the slight tingling prior to your departure from one world to another."

This comment also made Nina's mind whirl. "Different worlds?"

"The real world where you live and this magical world you are fortunate enough to visit."

"How does it work?" Questioned Nina before adding, "The piano wound itself up. What made that happen?"

Kumah had joined them and was bouncing up and down on the ground. "Does it matter? How about we go on an adventure and stop wasting time with the how and why's and just have some fun."

Nina agreed with Kumah. She had wasted enough time asking questions and now knowing she might have to leave at any moment meant there wasn't time to waste. Recalling her last visit to the ranch she asked, "Could we go see the waterfalls?"

"That's a splendid idea," Kumah replied. "How would you like to get there?"

Nina considered Kumah's question before answering, "I guess I can walk so Tarak doesn't have to carry me." Her answer made Kumah laugh so hard she rolled around on her back holding her wee little belly. Nina wasn't sure why her answer was so hilarious but hearing Kumah's adorable laughter made Nina join in.

Tarak cleared his throat which instantly brought Kumah to attention. In a calm tone Tarak coaxed, "Pretend Nina. Use your imagination and think of way to travel that you can't do at home. Something only dreams are made of."

"Something fun!" added Kumah bouncing on her back legs.

Nina's mind swirled with thoughts quickly landing on one specific idea brought on by Gram's words. Even before she could speak the words she was floating above the ground. Instinctively she stretched out her arms, leaned to the right and off she went. Soaring above the ground was a freeing experience. She went in circles first to the right and then the left. "I'm doing more than floating, I'm flying!" shrieked an exuberant Nina. "So much for gravity," laughed Nina. That's when she pulled her feet beneath her bringing her to a stop. "Come on guys. It's so much fun!"

Kumah didn't hesitate. She rocketed into the air laughing her enchanting laugh.

The two of them darted back and forth across the sky swirling around each other, touching the tip-top crown of the massive pine trees and swooping down on the meadow to let the tall grass tickle their tummies. It was a dream come true for Nina. She had forgotten all about going to see the waterfalls which Tarak soon reminded her of.

"Okay show me the way," encouraged Nina.

Tarak took a few steps forward saying, "Follow me."

Nina flew next to Tarak and stopped directly in front of him. "You're not going to fly?"

"I prefer to walk," replied Tarak.

Kumah whispered in Nina's ear, "It's not dignified enough for him to fly. We can just follow him from above."

Nina stood her ground, tilted her head and said, "Please Tarak." He didn't budge, but Nina was determined to get him to fly with her. An idea popped in her head, "You're my guardian Tarak, right?" although up to this point she had no clue as to why she needed a guardian.

"I am."

"Well doesn't it make sense for you to be as close to me as you can?"

"Agreed," confirmed a seemingly reluctant Tarak.

Nina swore she saw a twinkle in Tarak's eye despite his protest so she pressed on. "Then you have to fly with me to keep me safe," insisted Nina.

Tarak's sense of duty kicked into overdrive. Nina's safety trumped his reluctance to join them in the air. With a simple nod of his head he agreed then raced off across the meadow soon becoming airborne.

"He looks like one of Santa's reindeer," blurted Nina gleefully.

"Oh don't tell him that," Kumah urged.

"Okay, that'll be our little secret."

The next thing they knew Tarak zoomed past them instructing them to follow him. Nina and Kumah did as he ordered, but he was moving so fast Kumah had a hard time keeping up. Nina slowed down, grabbed Kumah in her hands and placed her in the shirt pocket of her pajama's. With Kumah safely tucked in her shirt Nina darted towards Tarak soon catching up to him.

The view from the sky held a beauty Nina had never seen. It appeared like the sky was never-ending while the landscape below them changed over and over again. Rolling green hills, wildflower filled meadows, dense patches of trees to crystal clear lakes where the fish would try and keep up with Nina as she flew by. It was better than any dream she had ever had. At last Nina spotted two rivers meandering through the green terrain. Nina noticed the earth disappeared in the distance and when she reached it she understood why.

Both rivers fell off the bluff creating separate and distinct waterfalls. Not long after each of the rivers completed its decent did their white-water crash into the other creating a narrow single river. Forced together between opposing walls of granite the rivers united racing full speed ahead. Soon the sound of a much larger waterfall reached Nina's ears. Tarak flew towards the roaring sound of cascading water. Nina soon followed. Upon reaching the breathtaking sight Nina levitated above the plunge pool admiring the beauty around her. The rapidly moving single river had separated again into two waterfalls. One was far larger then it's diminutive counterpart. Much of the rock formations were covered with overgrown brush. All the bushes and trees framing the magnificent water feature were so green it seemed like something from a cartoon. This color green didn't exist in the real world.

The spray of the water from the waterfall had Nina soaked in no time, so she decided to dive into the plunge pool. Laughing as she came up out of the water was music to Tarak's ears. He was now standing on the rocky bank surrounding the pool of water as it continued on its way down another tributary.

"Hello Nina," greeted a young fallfish.

"Hello," replied Nina even before she saw the fish. Once she caught sight of him she said, "The sun is making your back shine with golden sparkles and I love your big eyes."

The fish disappeared into the water making Nina fearful she had offended the little guy. He soon returned saying, "I needed some air."

With a sweet smile Nina replied, "That makes sense."

"Thank you for the compliments."

A terrible thought suddenly entered Nina's mind. If the fish needed air so did Kumah who was still in Nina's pocket. Nina felt for Kumah in her pocket then the other one thinking she was mistaken about which pocket she had put her little friend into, but she wasn't there. Frantically she searched the water's surface for Kumah in hopes she could swim. Nothing. Before Nina could spiral out of control Tarak calmly said, "I have her."

Nina looked over at Tarak and spotted Kumah clinging to his antlers. "Are you alright?" asked a still terrified Nina.

"I'm okay," I flew over to Tarak before you dove in. I don't like water except to drink," teased Kumah.

Relief washed over Nina like never before. It took a few moments for her racing heart to slow down, but when it did Nina went back to enjoying this remarkable experience. She and the little fish whose name was Gilly had a rather lengthy conversation in between his dives for air. Nina floated on her back staring up at the intensely blue sky. Every color in this magical realm was fiercely more profound than any colors at home. It made the real world seen bland and dull.

Boom!!! Nina landed hard on her bedroom floor. A bit off balance she placed her hand on her dresser to steady herself when she stood up. She was home, much to her dismay. Feeling stable she made her way to her bedroom window where her dad was still cutting the grass and she noticed he wasn't even halfway done. Nina's mom on the other hand was heading for the garage. Soon Nina could hear her mom coming up the stairs.

Frightened about how she would explain why she was soaking wet she rushed to the bathroom and shut the door. That's when she noticed she was completely dry. Her mom knocked on the bathroom door saying, "Good morning."

"Good morning Mom," replied Nina trying to sound calm.

"After you have something to eat come outside with us please."

"Yes Mom."

Nina ate her bowl of cereal slowly. She was trying so hard to hold tight to the wonderful adventure she had experienced. Methodically she went through her time with Tarak and Kumah in an effort to forever lock away the memories. The clear winner of all that had taken place was the ability to fly. She put her bowl in the sink and went outside. Her dad had finished cutting the grass and her mom was busy trimming her roses. Nina had once thought they were the most colorful flowers she'd ever seen, but now they paled in comparison to the magical world.

In no time the entire family moved to the backyard where Nina helped by sweeping the patio. When the yard was completed they decided to go get some lunch. Thankfully her parents were too busy in their own conversation they failed to notice Nina was in a world all her own. Over and over she replayed the events of her enchanting morning. Each time bringing her back to one specific unforgettable sight. Nina was sure the sight of Tarak flying high in the air resembling one of Santa's reindeer would never fade. Just

picturing him soaring through the sky made her
giggle.

Code of Conduct

Much to Nina's dismay her family spent most of the next day away from home. What would have normally been an enjoyable weekend going to the movies, out for dinner and ice cream couldn't compare to her adventures with Tarak and Kumah. When Nina's mind wondered again her mom asked, "Nina, aren't you having fun?"

The look of disappointment on Valerie's face made Nina feel bad for being preoccupied all day long. Nina did her best to make amends, "I'm having fun Mom," but it didn't convince Valerie.

Once they arrived home Nina's mom readdressed the issue. "Is everything alright at school?" questioned Valerie while taking a seat on the edge of Nina's bed.

"Mom everything is fine," insisted Nina.

"Okay if you say so. You just didn't seem to be having as much fun as you usually do on our family days."

Ouch. That remark cut Nina to the core. With a big squeeze Nina hugged her mom doing her best to reassure Valerie all was well. They talked for a bit longer then said their traditional goodnight. Nina sensed her mom wasn't convinced and she wasn't sure how to fix it. No sooner was Valerie downstairs did Nina hear the faint sound of the music box playing.

Nina sat up in bed and in the blink of an eye found herself seated halfway up the steps at the ranch house. The night sky was filled with more stars then she'd ever seen and a cool gentle wind gave her a chill. Tarak was face to face with her and he wasted no time in speaking, "Nina you must learn to separate your visits here from your life at home."

Nina began, "But I....."

Tarak interrupted her with an even firmer tone, "No but's, no excuses Nina. If you can't find a way to exist in both worlds without making your parent's suspicious you will no longer be allowed to portal between worlds."

"Will the music box break again?"

"Either that or we will close and lock the gate between realms."

This unexpected news hit Nina like a ton of bricks. The mere thought of never returning to this magical world crushed her. Nina didn't know how she would do what Tarak was demanding of her, but she was determined to find a way. She asked with welling eyes, "Can you help me from having to stay away?"

Tarak remained on task without answering Nina's question. "What happens if your mom calls you when you're using your imagination to play with your toys at home?"

Nina answered with the obvious, "I stop using my pretend voices and talk to her normally."

Tarak urged her to continue by saying, "Then?"

"I either go back to playing or do whatever she asks me to do."

"Do you take your toys and imagination with you if you have to stop playing?"

"No, I put the toys away and just go back to life."

"Then think of this place the same way. When you leave, put us away like your other toys and rest assured we're safely inside the piano like a magical toy box."

"I'll try," agreed Nina wiping a single tear from her face.

Tarak gave her a stern look, "You can't just try Nina. It is essential that you keep the true magic of the music box hidden. You are required to do so without fail."

This matter was clearly of great importance. Nina could feel the weight of the situation as her heart grew heavy and her eyes overflowed with tears. Compelling her to do whatever needed to be done to keep the piano's magic from being discovered. Nina didn't know all the details why this was so important and she wasn't quite sure she wanted to know. Holding her head high with her shoulders back she made an oath, "I will keep the music box secret to myself. I cross my heart."

"That's my dear one," approved Tarak in a much more pleasant tone.

The cool evening breeze that was caressing Nina's face vanished. She was back in her bed still feeling the heaviness of her conversation with Tarak. He meant business and Nina knew it. A memory came rushing back of the time her father talked to her about strangers and dangers in the world. Marc had the same no nonsense tone and intensity in his eyes as he walked a fine line between making Nina aware of bad things without completely terrifying her. Tarak's assertive warning had made Nina feel uneasy just as her father's conversation had. That's the first-time Nina considered the possibility of the magical realm being anything but wonderful.

When morning arrived, Nina got ready for school and made sure when she came home it was like any other day. The fear of never traveling through the piano again frightened her, but not as much as what her imagination was dreaming up. Was there danger in the magical world? Could she destroy the magic by not keeping it a secret? Not wanting to let Tarak down Nina did as she was told. She pushed aside any thoughts of the music box, did her homework, helped her mom with dinner and went to bed without thinking of her great-grandma's music box for more than a second. It wasn't easy, but sheer determination for wanting to keep her friends in the magical world safe was motivation enough.

"I'm so very proud of you dear one," whispered Tarak.

Nina opened her weary eyes then rubbed them to clear her vision. Sure enough Tarak was standing over her with Kumah in his antlers. "Thank you," Nina murmured. It took Nina a few moments to fully wake up. When she did she was startled that the sun was high in the sky above her. Was she dreaming? Had she truly traveled through the gateway into the magical world?

The confusion was apparent on her face causing Kumah to try and help, "Time is different here than it is at your home."

This was something Nina had noticed, but she hadn't given any real thought to. She didn't care why or how she could return from a full day with her friends to find only a few minutes had passed at home. "I did kinda notice that. I guess it's a good thing. Am I dreaming?"

"No," smiled Kumah now sitting in Nina's hand. It only takes a single note to play from the piano for you to be transported here or there.

"Thankfully your parents are sound sleepers," added Tarak.

Nina had to know. "Did I do good today?"

"You did wonderful," Tarak answered in a dignified manner and yet his eyes were bursting with pride for her.

Relief washed over Nina's face before saying, "Thank you. It would be sad if I couldn't come back to...." that's when Nina realized she didn't know the name of this delightful place. "What's the name of this place?"

"Sovanna," replied Tarak in a clear deep voice full of reverence. Kumah also showed her respect by bowing her head.

Nina remained quiet until Kumah lifted her head then she whispered as low as she could, "Sovanna." She wasn't sure she was allowed to even say the name. Tarak was quick to tell her she could speak the word Sovanna without fear as long as she only spoke it when she was there. The rules for this dreamy place were starting to add up.

"Get some sleep Nina. We will see you soon," Tarak said and before her next breath Nina returned to her bed falling asleep in no time. A dream-filled night left her feeling groggy in the morning, so she told her mom she'd had a bad night's sleep because of a nightmare. Nina wasn't completely sure it was a lie because she couldn't recall much about her dreams. It was possible her dreams were scary.

As the weeks passed Nina figured there wasn't time to visit Sovanna. She missed her friends there, but life had gotten very busy. Between growing amounts of homework and fall soccer season starting there wasn't a lot of spare time. With each passing day Nina found herself feeling much better about keeping Sovanna a secret. She actually began to feel very special knowing she was the only one permitted to travel there.

It wasn't until evening on Thanksgiving that Nina visited Sovanna again. Standing on the top of a small hill she looked in all directions for anything she recognized. "Hello!" she shouted with her hands cupped around her mouth.

"Hello," replied a voice from above.

Nina turned around and spotted a dark long-haired creature with a furry tail lounging on a branch high in a tree. His round ears and face sort of reminded Nina of a bear, but he clearly wasn't a bear. The creature let his rear legs straddle the limb and dangle while his front legs held tight to the hefty branch. He was very long reminding Nina of an otter, but he didn't have an adorable friendly face. When he opened his mouth to speak all Nina could see was a mouth full of sharp white teeth. His four fang-like teeth held her focus. She was sure when the two on the top met the two on the bottom it would pierce whatever it was biting. Preoccupied by the thought of being bit by this animal Nina missed what he had said.

"Did you hear me?" hissed the animal now standing on all fours.

"No, I'm sorry I was wondering something," Nina replied thinking quick on her feet.

"What were you thinking?" he called Nina's bluff.

Without hesitation Nina spoke the truth, "I was wondering what kind of animal you are."

"That's of no importance," was all he said before repeating what Nina had missed, "Are you the famous Nina I've heard so much about?"

"Famous?" Nina mumbled to herself. "I'm not famous, but my name is Nina. What is your name?"

"My name is Amos."

"It's nice to meet you," smiled Nina trying to hide her wariness.

Amos seemed to be smirking at Nina when he asked, "Would you like to go on an adventure with me?"

"No, she will not go on an adventure with you," Tarak cautioned standing between Nina and Amos.

The two glared at each other for such a long-time Nina found herself drawing closer to Tarak. She stroked Tarak's side with a shaky hand hoping he would take it as a sign for them to leave.

Amos crept down from the tree before disappearing into the tall grass scoffing, "All in good time," as the tree vanished before their eyes.

That's when another new voice caught Nina's attention. She looked up and there seated on Tarak's back was a young girl about Nina's age. She had dark hair and eyes like Nina's and there was something familiar about her. "Climb up Nina and Tarak will take us back to the ranch."

"I'd rather fly to get there faster," was all Nina could say as she soared into the air. Not sure which way to go she hovered in the sky and hollered, "Tarak please show me the way." That's when the young girl on his back waved. That was it! She was the young girl who had waved at her from the wagon and the back of the theater. Before Nina could say another word Tarak flew by with the young girl laughing contagiously as they flew towards the sun.

No sooner had they reached the ranch did Nina say, "You're the girl who kept waving at me," her excitement uncontainable.

"Yes I am."

"Who are you?"

"My friends call me Roo," which Nina figured was a nickname, but she didn't care, they were finally meeting.

In her excitement Nina failed to notice the sly look Tarak gave Roo. Kumah had joined them along with a bunch of other animals. There were far too many to meet individually so Roo simply said, "This is the gang. Say hello to Nina everyone."

In unison, the entirety of the mix-matched group said, "Nice to meet you Nina."

Nina replied in kind. There were smaller animals riding on larger animals, birds, owls, butterflies and even lady bugs flying above. Everywhere she looked there was some kind of creature happily smiling at her. Nina searched the crowd for Amos feeling a sense of relief when she didn't spot him.

"He is not allowed here," explained Tarak. "He wouldn't dare travel this close to the ranch. I'm actually surprised he ventured as far as he did from...." Tarak stopped before finishing his sentence then redirected his thoughts, "What fun should we have today?"

Roo agreed. She took Nina inside the ranch house for the first-time. The high wooden vaulted ceilings caught Nina's attention first. The floor was wood, the stairs leading upstairs were wood, all the wooden doors were framed in pretty carved wood and the walls were covered in stripped wallpaper. It was unlike any house Nina had ever been in. That's when she noticed the massive stone fireplace that swallowed up an entire wall. There was a large cast iron kettle hanging from a hook over the fire filling the entire room with a mouth-watering aroma.

"Lunch will be ready shortly, let's go play in my room," suggested an elated Roo. Although she appeared to be around Nina's age Roo spoke in a more formal manner.

"Sure," Nina agreed following her up the stairs.

There were stuffed animals covering the bed and a few ceramic dolls on a shelf. Nina was relieved to see they had cute baby-like faces unlike some she had seen in a thrift store with her mom. Those ones were a bit frightening which as far as Nina was concerned was why they hadn't been sold. Roo dumped a crate of blocks on the floor and said let's play with these first. Each block had a picture of half an animal on each side. Roo showed her how she could put a cow's face with a cat's body to make an imaginary animal. They laughed as they put blocks together creating animals that didn't exist, but it was fun to imagine. The real fun began when Roo put the correct pieces together.

When the animal blocks were as they should be, the animals came to life. First a seal, then a rooster, followed by a tiger and a horse. No matter how many or how big the animals they all fit in Roo's bedroom without a problem. No one fought, they all talked and laughed together. Whatever Roo or Nina imagined it came to life making their playtime unbelievably incredible. From below someone yelled, "The food is ready. Wash up and come down to eat."

After washing up they headed downstairs. When Nina was halfway down the steps she spotted a large white and gray wolf wearing an apron and standing on her hind legs. She placed two bowls on the large dining table. Then went back to the cabinets and pulled spoons from a drawer. Not only did the wolf hold the spoons she used a knife to butter the freshly baked bread for the girls. This was the most magically wonderful place Nina had ever been too and it kept getting better.

Nina took her seat, scooped the stew onto her spoon but before she could taste the food she found herself back in her room. Nina regretted she didn't get to eat her meal, but she knew there had to be a reason for her sudden return. The reason presented itself when her dad came into her room. He asked Nina if she wanted to go with him to the park while Valerie enjoyed some alone time after preparing yesterday's Thanksgiving meal.

Agreeing to go Nina got ready and tucked her adventures with Roo in her heart. Roo was a new friend, but there was already a uniquely strong connection between them. She had almost forgotten about meeting Amos, but even when he crossed her mind she believed Tarak would protect her. With her whole heart Nina believed Tarak would keep her from harm.

Questions Multiply

Upon reaching the park Nina spotted her grandma waiting at a picnic table with a basket. Grandma had missed spending Thanksgiving with the family because she had spent Thanksgiving with an old friend who was terribly ill. Nina ran to her grandma repeatedly yelling, "Grandma!" until she was wrapped in Theresa's arms.

"Why didn't mom come?" Nina asked her dad.

"She needs some rest angel, so we thought this was a good idea," Marc answered giving Theresa a wink.

Grandma started unloading the picnic basket. There were egg salad sandwiches, a few chip selections and freshly baked chocolate chip cookies for dessert. They shared their yummy meal while Marc and Grandma discussed her visit with her sick friend, who thankfully was doing better. After finishing her sandwich and chips Nina ate two of the gooey cookies, making sure to eat any crumbs that fell on her paper plate then headed to the playground. Grandma and Marc remained at the picnic table keeping an eye on Nina while they continued their conversation. Nina didn't care what the adults were talking about she was too busy having fun with the other children at the park. If she had known what the topic of conversation was she would have probably chosen to stay with Grandma and Dad.

By the time Nina and her dad returned home they found Valerie sound asleep on the couch with a half-opened book still in her hand. Marc skillfully removed the book from his wife's hand, then pulled the fleece blanket up to cover her shoulders. After a quick search Marc took some hamburgers outside to barbecue requesting Nina join him. He grilled some onions and sweet peppers to put on the burgers and just as he placed the buns on the barbecue to lightly toast them rain began to fall.

"It's raining," exclaimed Nina, excited to see the first rainfall of the season. She didn't have to ask her dad; he knew exactly what she wanted. Quietly she went inside and put on her rain coat, hat and boots before returning outside to splash around in the growing puddles. Marc told her she could play outside if she was quiet and he'd bring her food out to her. While Valerie continued to sleep Marc and Nina enjoyed their dinner under the patio cover. Nina enjoyed her rather plain cheeseburger, just a bun, burger with melted cheese and a little ketchup. She did however ask for seconds of the baked beans. When finished with their food they remained seated and watched the increasing downpour plummet from the sky. The backyard lights lit up the raindrops making them look like white streaks racing to the ground.

Shortly after a flash of lightning lit up the night sky a deafening thunderclap rumbled overhead. It was time to go inside. Valerie had been startled awake by the booming thunder and was sitting up when her family came in. "Are you hungry?" asked Marc.

Valerie thought about this, which made no sense to Nina. Why wouldn't her mom know if she were hungry? Valerie finally said, "A little. I should try and eat something."

While Marc made his wife a plate he instructed Nina to go get her pajama's on since it was getting close to bedtime. By the time she finished getting ready for bed and came downstairs Valerie was still eating. Nina watched her mom take the tiniest of bites, chew slowly before swallowing and then wait an odd amount of time before taking another itsy-bitsy bite.

"Are you okay Mom?" questioned Nina thinking something was amiss.

"Yes, I'm fine bumblebee. I just feel really tired."

Marc intervened, "Your mom is just tired from all her hard work yesterday."

That seemed like a reasonable explanation thought Nina. She kissed her mom goodnight per Marc's request before he took her upstairs to tuck her in for the night. The sound of the steady rain lulled Nina to sleep within minutes. When morning rolled around she could smell pancakes and bacon wafting up the stairs. As soon as she brushed her teeth she rushed downstairs. Instead of finding her mom in the kitchen it was her dad. He greeted her with a hug and kiss before asking her how many pancakes and pieces of bacon she wanted.

She answered him then asked where her mom was. Marc told her Mom was still sleeping. This was curious since Valerie was usually the first one up. "Isn't she going to eat breakfast with us?" Nina inquired.

"I'm not sure angel," answered Marc pouring the syrup over Nina's pancakes.

"Breakfast smells amazing mi amor," said Valerie coming down the stairs.

"Good morning Mom," cheered Nina feeling much better after seeing her mom join them.

Nina kept her eyes on her mom as they began to eat their breakfast. Valerie was eating normally unlike last night so Nina figured everything was back to normal. She told her mom all about her picnic with Grandma and Dad as well as all the fun she had playing with the other kids. Of course, the highlight from the previous day was splashing around in last night's rainstorm and listening to the thunder which Nina loved. Most kids are afraid of thunder and lightning. It's the rare child who finds amusement in the bright flashes of light and the powerful rumble of thunder. Nina was one such child. As far back as they could remember Nina would stop whatever she was doing to listen for the next thunderous boom. Even if she were crying over something Nina would stop and sit quietly. She wouldn't move as she waited with eager anticipation for the next roll of thunder. When it finally roared through the sky Nina would laugh and when old enough she would jump up and down saying, "Boom, boom."

Valerie chuckled at Nina's recollection of the day before. After apologizing for being so tired and missing out on all the fun Nina's mom asked her, "Grandma wants to know if you want to go spend today and tomorrow with her since she had to miss Thanksgiving with us." Nina wholeheartedly agreed to go spend the night at her grandmas. Grandma always played games, did crafts and colored with Nina making the day's lots of fun. It would be the first-time Nina had spent the night at Grandma's new home which made it even more exciting.

"Well see you tomorrow," assured Valerie when she and Marc dropped Nina off.

"Okay Mom," Nina replied anxious to get started on the fun.

The first order of business once inside Grandma's house was for Theresa to show Nina something. There was a small room off the living room that could be used for an office, but in anticipation of her granddaughter spending the night Theresa had turned it into a guest room. Nina was delighted to see what Grandma had done for her. Front and center was a full-size bed with a fabric covered arched canopy. The light and airy cloth was a pale pink covered with white polka dots. The walls were a soft gray with pictures of farm animals on one wall while on either side of the window were flower photos. Nina's favorite thing in her room were the stenciled butterflies flying out from behind the headboard up towards the ceiling where a few actually were. Grandma pointed out a toy box in one corner of the room which was overflowing with toys. In another corner was a bookcase with a mixture of books and stuffed animals lining the shelves.

"Thank you Grandma!" squealed an exhilarated Nina. "It's so pretty," she continued hugging her grandma.

"You're very welcome jellybean. It's your own little space when you visit."

By the time the sun sat the two of them had played games, gone for a walk, made three different crafts and colored. Grandma ordered pizza so she didn't have to waste time cooking. She felt her time was better spent with Nina. While they sat at the dinner table and ate their dinner Grandma asked, "Are you enjoying the music box?"

Nina's face lit up with delight, "I am! I love the song it plays. Did you know my mom and dad dance to that song on their anniversary?"

Theresa couldn't help but smile brightly at her granddaughter's enthusiasm. "I did know that." Grandma wasn't sure if Nina thought it was their wedding anniversary, but it didn't matter.

The night Marc proposed was well worth celebrating and Nina was so proud of knowing it was a special day.

Nina took another bite of her pizza and watched as Theresa stared off into the distance. When she turned back to face Nina her eyes looked sad for some reason. Nina asked, "Are you going to cry?"

"No jellybean. I was just remembering playing with my mom, your great-grandma as a little girl. We would spend hours listening to the music box play."

Nina blurted the words, "Play me a tale," regretting she hadn't been more careful. Was she putting all her magical friends in danger?

Theresa's eyes changed to that of fond remembrance as she responded, "Yes jellybean. Play me a tale. It was what your great-grandma would tell me to say before we went on our adventures. No matter what we played after I said those magic words it would come to life." Nina's heart raced at the thought of her great-grandma and grandma playing at the ranch or knowing

Tarak and Kumah, but that feeling left with Grandma's next words, "Well at least I thought those words were magical when I was little. Now I know better." That's when Theresa saw disappointment in Nina's eyes.

"Oh, I'm sorry jellybean. What I meant to say was, as an adult I just don't have the imagination I did when I was a child. How I wish I did. Me and my mother had so much fun and they are some of my very favorite memories."

Knowing more about the magical world Nina thought of a good question to ask. "Is losing your imagination why the music box broke?" Keeping her following thoughts to herself Nina wondered. Did Grandma stop believing in magic or had the piano been broken by Tarak because Theresa had done something she shouldn't have?

"No, it still played music but I never went on another adventure."

Nina continued with her line of questioning. "How did it break?"

"I don't remember. That was a long time ago."

"Did my mom play with it?"

"She did when she was a little older then you."

Perhaps Nina's mom had done something to break the box. Was Valerie guilty of not keeping the piano's secret? "Did you guys go on adventures with each other?" asked a curious Nina.

"Of course we did. We would spend a lot of time playing together with the music box and using our imaginations." That's when forgotten memories rushed in. Theresa recalled countless fun-filled times with Valerie as a child, causing Theresa's eyes to well with happy tears. Grandma continued, "I would tell your mom some of my experiences with your great-grandma. Of course, I played along when your mom used the piano. Those are some of my favorite memories with your mom. Thank you for helping me remember them."

Then Nina questioned, "Did you go with my mom when she used her imagination?"

Grandma chose her words carefully, not wanting to hinder Nina's imaginative play, "I pretended to see what she was seeing, but I guess I outgrew the magic."

"That's sad," remarked Nina hoping she would never outgrow the music box's magic.

"It is sad," concurred Theresa who then asked, "Have you had any magical playtime now that the music box is working? Have you said Play me a tale?"

Nina was concerned about saying the wrong thing. She also wondered why it had taken so long for anyone to ask if she had used the words "Play me a tale" when listening to the music box. If Grandma and Mom had such pleasant memories of their adventures why hadn't they asked Nina if she was having as much fun as they once had?

Saved by the bell for the very first-time made sense to Nina. Before she had time to answer Grandma's question her doorbell rang. It was a neighbor wanting to borrow a few eggs. Grandma gave them to her after introducing the woman to Nina. The lady had a thick accent

166

making it hard for Nina to understand. Theresa was a big help in playing translator between the two.

After the woman left Nina asked, "You don't have a hard time knowing what she's saying?"

"I had a little trouble when we first met, but I'm pretty good with accents, even ones I've never heard. I figured it out soon enough."

"I'm not good with accents," confessed Nina before yawning.

"Perhaps you should get to bed. We've had a very busy day."

It was a little earlier than Nina went to bed, but concern over giving something away about the piano helped her agree with Grandma. Theresa read Nina one of her favorite books before tucking her in. "Sleep well and I'll see you in the morning."

"Goodnight Grandma," yawned Nina feeling happy that she was in bed. Drifting off to sleep came quickly and easily. Even the different noises in Grandma's house didn't disturb Nina's slumber. Her dreams were filled with normal kid stuff.

Playing with friends, flying kites with her mom and dad, but her final dream frightened her awake. Nina popped up in bed realizing that daybreak had come, which helped her brush off the nightmare she was having. Part of her wanted to remember what scared her but a bigger part of her didn't.

Nina could hear her grandma bustling around in the kitchen. When Nina made her way there Theresa was drinking her coffee while mixing waffle batter. "Did you sleep well?"

"Yep," Nina answered trying to forget being jolted awake.

"Good. Go get washed up. I'll have the waffles made in no time."

Ups and Downs

Nina's family enjoyed a relaxing dinner. Marc had smoked tri-tip all day, one of Nina's favorites, and served it alongside some mac and cheese, corn on the cob and buttered rolls. As she ate Nina told her parents all about her room at Grandma's and all the fun they had. They smiled at her animation as she shared stories about her time at Grandma's.

Valerie tucked Nina into bed after laying out her school clothes for the next day and went to bed herself. Marc stayed up and got some work done in anticipation for a meeting he had later that week. Nina was restless during the night as her mind raced with more and more questions about the music box and whether a time would come when she would no longer be able to travel between worlds.

The weeks leading up to Christmas break were packed full of fun activities at school. There were countless rehearsals for the schools Christmas concert and Nina's favorite event was approaching. A shopping day at the school just for the students.

Impatiently Nina waited her turn to enter the Christmas boutique. The helpers dressed as elves took each student's shopping form with instructions on who to buy for and how much money to spend. After verifying payment was included in the envelope stapled to the instruction form each child began their shopping. A certain number of students were allowed in the shop at a time to keep things organized. When Nina was next in line she tried to spot gift possibilities for her parents and grandma. She quickly noticed a little figurine of an angel holding a heart in her hands, there were words written on the angels dress but she couldn't make them out. How she hoped it would be a fitting gift for her mom.

"My name is Holly and I'll be your elf shopper. What is your name?"

"Nina," replied an excited Nina handing the cheerful elf her shopping form. As the elf lead Nina into the library her heart sank. The angel she had been admiring was no longer on the table. "It's gone," mumbled a heartbroken Nina.

"What's gone?" inquired Holly.

"There was a little angel statue on that table but it's gone."

"Well, let's see if I can help," suggested Holly leading Nina towards the table she was pointing to. "Miss Cookie I was wondering if you have any more angel figurines."

Miss Cookie had very short hair and frameless glasses that she looked over the top of at Holly. The wrinkles around her face and eyes grew more evident when she smiled at Nina saying, "Are you looking for something for your mother?" No sooner did Nina answer did Miss Cookie turn around and open a box. She lifted a box with a picture of the angel on it. "I was just about to set some more of these out. Holly would you open this one and make sure it's not broken while I gather a few more?"

Holly carefully opened the box and unwrapped the figurine from its layers of tissue paper, then after a thorough examination happily announced, "It's in perfect condition. Is this what you would like to get your mom?"

Nina asked to see the angel so she could read the writing. Reading out loud Nina said, "World's Best Mom."

Holly confirmed she had enough money to purchase the item then with great care she rewrapped the gift and had Miss Cookie re-tape the box closed. Then it was off to find her dad and grandma some gifts. Nina found a pale blue coffee cup with a daisy on it and the words "Wonderful Grandma" written under the flower. There were a few items Nina was debating about getting her dad. She finally decided the one she wanted was a miniature street sign that said "Dad's BBQ Way" on it. Her dad's love of barbecuing was the clear winner over all the other gift options. There was even enough money left for Nina to get herself some Christmas cookies.

When Nina was picked up from school she held tight to the bag with her gifts. She was careful not to give the slightest hint on what she had purchased. "I want it to be a surprise for everyone," Nina stated, although keeping her gifts for Marc and Theresa a secret from her mom was killing her. She desperately wanted to show her mom what a great job she did, but she fought against that impulse. Once home she asked her mom for some wrapping paper, bows and name tags. Nina was hoping that once the presents were wrapped and under the tree she would no longer feel the need to share what any of them were.

Nina had never wrapped presents before, but she did her best. When finished with her wrapping everything was hidden under the green paper with Santa and his reindeers frolicking in the falling snow. Nina didn't know it, but the excessive amount of tape she had used would prove to make opening her gifts on Christmas morning a bit challenging. Not wanting to risk dropping a gift Nina made three trips down and back up the stairs. Grandma's gift was the last and she placed it on the dining table before saying, "Mom, I need help spelling grandma."

Valerie spelt out grandma while Nina intently focused on fitting the word on the small name tag. Fearing she was running out of room Nina started making the letters smaller and smaller. The last two letters ended up below the rest of the letters making Nina look less than happy. "Bumblebee, Grandma won't mind how her name looks. She'll be so proud of you for filling out the tag on your own. That's all she'll care about. You did a great job wrapping your own gifts."

"Thanks. It'll be thrown away with the wrapping paper anyways and wait till Grandma sees what I got her," Nina said trying to convince herself that her sloppy job of writing grandma didn't matter.

"Exactly."

Nina placed the final present under the tree. Joining her mom on the couch she asked, "Mom did you stop playing with the music box because it broke?" Nina had been wondering about this ever since her last visit with Grandma.

"I did. It made me very sad when it broke and Grandma tried several different places to get it repaired, but no one was able to fix it."

"How did it break?" pressed Nina.

Valerie shrugged her shoulders and said, "I don't know, none of us do. It was working one day and the next it wasn't."

Nina was afraid to mention Tarak and Kumah so she decided on a way around it. "Grandma said you used to say 'Play me a tale' and have adventures like she did when she was little."

"I did have magical adventures," agreed Valerie whose face lit up. "I remember playing tea party with my toys and saying those magic words. My dolls and stuffed animals came to life and even the tea was real. Tea party had always been one of my favorite things to play, but when it magically came to life it became the only thing I wanted to play."

Excited to hear her mom talk about her magical playtime Nina asked, "So where else did you go besides your bedroom?"

Valerie's face showed bewilderment. "I didn't go anywhere all the make-believe fun took place in my bedroom. It was a lot of fun, but it was just a child's overactive imagination. There's no way those memories are real. It was just the power of suggestion or a child's creative way of passing the time." Valerie bit her tongue keeping herself from saying what she was thinking. Telling her daughter that magic wasn't real would spoil her momentary fun with the music box.

Nina knew her mother didn't lie to her, but how could she say the things she was saying? Why did Valerie and Theresa think the magic they had experienced wasn't real? What happened to make them no longer look back on those enchanted times as things that really did happen? The more answers Nina got the less she understood.

Doing her best to make amends Valerie asked, "Have you had any adventures with the music box?"

Nina didn't know what to say. If she told her mom about her time with Gram and being at the ranch with Tarak, would that cause something bad to happen? As she mulled over what if anything she should say, her mom gave her a way out, believing Nina had yet to have any magical experiences. Valerie suggested they go upstairs and she would wind up the music box for Nina. After the piano was fully wound Valerie kissed Nina on the cheek and went downstairs to start dinner. She turned around at the doorway and encouraged her daughter, "Don't forget to say 'Play me a tale' then watch what happens." Valerie sounded sincere, but Nina was puzzled. If her mom didn't think her experiences were real any more than Grandma did, why even try?

Waiting to hear her mom in the kitchen Nina then stated boldly, "Play me a tale."

As those words hung in the air Nina found herself standing at the base of the waterfalls she and Tarak had flown to. Although the water was still flowing the ground beneath Nina's feet was covered in snow. There were icicles hanging from some of the branches near the falls and patches of snow covered the pine trees. That's when she noticed her clothing had changed. She was wearing a blue button down coat with fur on the cuffs and collar. Nina noticed the matching gloves and boots on her hands and feet, then upon removing the beanie from her head she realized the beanie also matched. Her legs were covered in what looked and felt like thick black leggings. She wasn't the slightest bit cold even though she could see her breath upon greeting Tarak who stood proudly on the other side of the partly frozen plunge pool.

Tarak floated over to Nina and said, "It's so nice to see you dear one. It's been far too long."

"It has. I've missed coming here. Why haven't I been brought here?" Nina inquired as more questions raced through her head. Other than today she had only used the phrase "Play me a tale" one other time. She had visited Sovanna several times without saying that magical phrase.

"I had some business to attend to. I need to make sure you are always safe when you arrive." There was something in Tarak's explanation that worried Nina. She had almost forgotten about Amos and how he had frightened her.

Nina would have asked him more about this, but she had other pressing issues to address. "Why don't my grandma or mom believe they were actually here?"

"I'll explain all that I can, but first let's get inside. A storm is coming," instructed Tarak bending low so Nina could climb on. He didn't take to the air, instead he headed across the patches of ice towards the waterfall. Terrified she was about to be drenched in freezing cold water Nina squealed and covered her head with her arms. Not that her effort to keep herself from getting wet would have worked. With closed eyes Nina waited for the shock of being hit with rushing near freezing water, but when it didn't happen she peered through one eye.

A couple of pale turquoise pools caught Nina's attention and she quickly opened both her eyes. The water was so clear she could see all the way to the bottom of them. The tawny colored rock formations varied from rugged sharp edges to almost glassy smooth surfaces from decades of water rushing over them. Stalactites hung from the ceiling in a desperate attempt to reach the glistening water. Although they were clearly in a cave it was lit up giving Nina the illusion that they were standing in the sun.

"It's so beautiful!" exclaimed Nina having never been in a cave before, especially a mystical one.

"Yes, it is," Tarak agreed.

"I guess I should have known I wasn't going to get wet."

Tarak nodded before asking Nina to take a seat on a cushioned chair that appeared out of nowhere. As Nina sat down a table materialized before her. On it sat a cup of hot cocoa with miniature marshmallows and a plate lined with slices of warm banana bread. "Neither your grandma or mom ever came to Sovanna." Nina started to interrupt but Tarak's stern expression made her sit quietly. "There are very few that are given permission to enter Sovanna. Most, like your grandma and mom have much different encounters with magic and as they grow they stop believing in the piano's magic making it impossible to have any further escapades."

"Will I stop believing?" asked a fearful Nina. Then another question popped in her head,

"Maybe Grandma and Mom stopped believing because they never came to Sovanna."

Tarak answered Nina's first question, "It's highly doubtful that you will stop believing dear one, but not entirely impossible."

"I don't want to stop believing," stressed Nina almost knocking over her hot cocoa and forgetting about her second question.

Tarak hoped for the same chiming in, "I too hope you never stop believing."

Nina began to wonder if there was anyone who never stopped believing, but before she could finish that thought another subject matter came to mind. "Why did the piano break? Did my mom do something wrong?" How she hoped Tarak would say no to the latter question.

"The piano broke to keep it safe until you came along dear one. Your mom didn't do anything wrong, she merely stopped believing in the magic of the music box."

"That's why neither of them believe the magic ever really happened," groaned Nina feeling awful that her mom and grandma stopped believing in something so wonderful.

"That is correct," Tarak conceded. He walked closer to Nina and with a bow of his head declared, "We have been waiting a very long time for you dear one."

"You've been waiting for me?"

Tarak replied with a twinkle in his eyes, "Yes."

"Wait, you said we have been waiting. Who is we?"

"That is for another day and time. Right now, you must return home."

"So soon? Why?" pleaded Nina not at all ready to go home. "Can't I stay for just a little bit longer?"

Tarak never got to answer or wanted to answer. Nina found herself back in her parent's room angry for being sent back so soon, as well as Tarak not answering most of her questions.

Fears Come to Life

The music box was still playing so Nina climbed up on her parent's bed to finish listening to the pretty melody play out. No sooner did she make herself comfortable in the pile of decorative pillows did she hear little voices coming closer. "She's up here!" whooped a high-pitched squeal.

"There you are Nina," replied an elated stuffed unicorn who was quickly joined by most of Nina's stuffed animals. Many climbed onto Nina's lap until there wasn't any more room, making the others lie next to her. Then there were those who made their way up the pillows to sit near her head. A chubby fluffy white cat sat directly in front of Nina and said, "Could we play restaurant?"

"Sure, let's go back to my room where my kitchen set is," suggested Nina, but before she could make a move she noticed something astonishing. Her dishes, pots and pans and even her little stove and refrigerator filled with toy food making their way towards her. Before long Nina pretended to be the waitress serving food and drinks to all her little playmates. All of them except for the pudgy cat took turns being a waiter or waitress.

"Nina put your toys away and wash up for dinner," Valerie shouted from downstairs.

"Okay Mom," answered Nina. That's when she noticed the toys were putting themselves away. When the unicorn jumped into Nina's toy box the piano music ceased. Nina appreciated the toys putting themselves away, what a wonderful little bonus to her magical play.

"That was quick. Are you sure you put everything away?" questioned Valerie.

With an excited smile Nina answered, "They put themselves away so I just had to wash up." It felt so good for Nina to finally share a magical experience with her mom.

Her mom smiled an endearing smile at her daughter and said, "So you had a magical adventure?"

"I did," exclaimed a joyful Nina.

"I'm so happy for you bumblebee," replied Valerie. She didn't believe the toys had put themselves away, but either way she was sure they were put away and if pretending the toys were doing it themselves helped Nina clean up, so be it.

"Me too," agreed Nina. Her reply wasn't just because of the fun she'd had with her toys after they came to life, but also because she now had a magical event she wasn't afraid of sharing with her parents.

That night Nina rested peacefully. Her dreams were filled with incredible happenings with her toys, some even included her mom and grandma joining in the fun. Nina found herself much happier in the following days as the weight of keeping Sovanna a secret diminished. She happily continued to have magical episodes at home like her grandma and mom had done. Valerie even played along a few times and although she couldn't see the animals move around or hear them talk she pretended just the same. Nina found the entire thing quite entertaining. Her toys helped with the creativity of their playtime by giving Nina suggestions. Of course, Valerie simply thought it was Nina's inventive imagination coming up with the extremely intriguing ideas.

By the time her school's Christmas concert rolled around Nina was thoroughly enjoying her magical playtime.   Nina wondered with great anticipation how much more fun she would have during the Christmas break. She could play and amuse herself all day. A part of her missed Sovanna and its inhabitants, but having the weight of keeping that part of the music box's power hidden had taken a toll on her. There were too many unanswered questions. For now, she'd enjoy the make-believe play at home, even if she were the only one to actually see the magic.

Perhaps it was due to Nina thinking about those unanswered questions that caused that evenings nightmare. Coming up with her own answers to the unknowns proved futile. Was she making things far worse than they needed to be by fabricating her own conclusions? Or even worse, was the truth more terrifying than anything she could dream up? Not long after Nina had drifted off to sleep did she begin to dream. It started off innocent enough, but that didn't last long.

Nina was once again standing at the base of the waterfalls. The snow was gone and spring flowers covered the ground. The sweet aroma of the blossoms tickled Nina's nose. After greeting Nina with a splash of his tail Gilly and Nina shared stories of how they spent the winter. Deep in conversation neither of them noticed Amos approaching through the dense brush. When he was only a couple feet away Amos hissed like an angry cat drawing their attention to his arrival.

"It's been far too long Nina," remarked Amos. That simple statement felt less than kind. The spooky tone with which Amos spoke and his eerie grin left Nina feeling threatened.

Gilly fled underneath the water's surface leaving Nina alone. How she hoped Tarak would make an appearance, but as the seconds passed her hoped dwindled. "I was just leaving," stated Nina hoping those words alone would take her home or to the ranch, but nothing happened.

Amos crept closer and asked, "How about we go explore some of my favorite places?" he suggested before pausing to lick his back. After several moment's he raised his face to her and asked, "I'm ready, are you?"

"No!" shrieked Nina jumping into the air only to land hard on the ground beneath her. She couldn't fly away and she didn't understand why.

Amos laughed at her with a sinister laugh. "I'm in charge Nina."

Nina wished there were a phrase like "Play me a tale" that would take her home, but she didn't know one. In a feeble attempt Nina yelled, "Play me a tale," crossing her fingers that it would work. Her poor attempt to escape only made Amos's devious laugh grow louder.

Nina fought back tears and doing her best to seem brave she stood tall before turning to walk away. She took several steps making her feel confident in being able to get away, but a couple steps later caused her surroundings to change. Nina found herself back on the hilltop where she had first met Amos. This time he wasn't in a tree, he stood on his hind legs and gestured with his arm saying, "Let's go." Nina watched as his body turned to the left following his extended arm. Amos clearly wanted her to accompany him. Before turning his head to look where it was he wanted Nina to go, a wicked smirk crossed his face.

Nina gazed beyond Amos. She watched in horror as the dense forest behind him began to morph into a disturbing scene. A chill ran up Nina's spine watching the shimmering sunrays breaking through the trees grow dim. The colorful blossoms and the bright green ferns covering the ground were fading away. Fog started to roll in from all sides, the petals from the flowers dropped to the now barren ground and the trees no longer had leaves. How quickly the welcoming forest became a menacing dark and shadowy woodland. Way off in the distance Nina spotted flickering lights making their way through the trees. The yellowish tint of the glowing lights bobbed in weird patterns. Nina couldn't tell who or what was carrying them or if whatever was bringing them closer was walking, flying or hopping. As the lanterns came closer Nina felt a wave of fear engulf her like never before.

Nina couldn't move. Her feet felt glued to the ground, when she tried to cover her face with her hands she realized her arms wouldn't move nor could she make a sound. Tears streaming down her face only caused the dreadful scene before her to become even more ghastly. Never before had Nina felt this level of fear. Thankfully she managed to close her eyes in a last-ditch effort to shield herself from what was coming towards her.

Nina jumped as she felt someone's hands grab hold of her shoulders. "Nina, wake up you're having a bad dream." It was her dad's voice. Still unsure if it was truly her dad Nina tried to pull away from the grip that held her. Was Amos pretending to be her dad? Marc pulled his daughter into his arms and the scent of her father's cologne forced her to open her eyes. Through her teary eyes she could see she was back in her bedroom. Nina hugged her dad tightly feeling safe at last. With soothing reassurance

Marc calmed his sobbing daughter. "There you go angel. Your safe." Nina nodded in the affirmative, still too shaken to speak.

Valerie chimed in, "That must have been quite the nightmare, but it was just a bad dream Nina. Dreams can't hurt you," she added trying to ease her daughter's fear.

"Are you feeling better?" asked Marc.

Nina mumbled, "A little." Valerie's last comment actually did the opposite of what she intended. Nina knew Amos wasn't a dream and she believed hurting her was exactly what he wanted.

"Well grab your pillow and blanket and you can sleep on our floor. It's almost morning," suggested her mom.

That sounded like a good plan so Nina did as her mom suggested. Feeling safe with her parents sleeping near her and exhausted from her bad dream Nina surprisingly went back to sleep without much effort.

"Hello dear one," welcomed Tarak.

Nina scanned her surroundings. She was back in the cave with Tarak. The beauty of the secluded cave was even more grand. It seemed bigger with several more ponds of turquoise water. During her examination of her surroundings Nina noticed a tunnel at the far end of the cave. She couldn't recall it being there before. "Where's the tunnel go?" Nina questioned sounding a bit insistent.

There was no answer from Tarak. Eventually Nina moved her eyes from the tunnel back to Tarak. He stood there in his typical distinguished stance and cleared his throat. That was enough of a hint for Nina to grasp he wasn't going to answer her question and she knew why.

"I'm sorry Tarak," thinking a simple rather hollow apology would make amends. A somewhat humbler Nina then said, "Hello Tarak." Clearly her greeting wasn't enough as Tarak remained unwavering in his silence. Nina tried to remember what her mom would say to her when she was rude. Then it came to her, "I forgot my manners Tarak. I am very sorry."

"That's better," was all he said.

Nina wasn't sure why Tarak appeared to be so very agitated with her. Sure, she had forgotten to greet him before asking a question in an extremely rude manner, but after the nightmare she'd already had that night what did he expect? Perhaps there was something more to his behavior. Wanting to know if she had made a mistake or broken a rule she asked, "Did I do something wrong?"

Tarak's eyes softened before answering. "You didn't necessarily do something wrong and it wasn't entirely your fault, but it was a very close call."

Nina agreed it had been a close call. She couldn't hold back and launched into her nightmare with Amos, but the look on Tarak's face persuaded her to believe he already knew about it. She stopped halfway through her story and asked, "Were you there?"

"I was not," replied Tarak. Before Nina could pick up where she had left off on her story Tarak continued, "I do however know what happened."

Nina breathed a sigh of relief. The last thing she wanted to do was relive her nightmare. "Who is he? Why is there scary stuff here and why didn't you help me?"

In an extremely calm voice Tarak explained, "Amos is the manifestation of your fears."

"Manifestion?" Nina tried to repeat Tarak's word.

Tarak tried to explain Amos in another way, "Think of him as a living creature filled with your fears."

Another voice joined the conversation, "He's all the things you're afraid of wrapped up inside an animal," added Kumah.

"I don't want him here," protested Nina.

"None of us do," sympathized Tarak. "That is why I'm meeting with you at this precise moment."

Kumah jumped onto Nina's lap in an effort to comfort her as she sat quietly waiting for Tarak to continue telling her what he needed to say. He started off explaining that everyone has fears, even parents, which Nina had never considered.

Kumah shared some of her fears trying to help. Then Tarak went on to say fears are a normal part of life before moving on to the unpleasant facts of fears in Sovanna.

"Sovanna is a wonderful place. It can be filled with happy astonishing experiences making dreams come true," Tarak paused and when he continued speaking his tone grew cautious. "My dear one you have a fun carefree imagination, but deep within your mind there are also very real fears. Those fears come to life in Sovanna in a way they can't in your world. Amos wants to replace all your wonderful adventures here with scary monstrous adventures; although calling them adventures is less than accurate. We must stop him from changing Sovanna from a place where wondrous dreams come true to a place that is cursed and filled with never-ending torments for all who live and come here."

Nina was terrified by this new information. How could she or anyone else stop Amos? She couldn't even move the last time they were face to face. Crying for the first-time in Sovanna Nina asked, "How do we stop him?"

"Have no fear dear one, it's been done before," comforted Tarak.

"It has?" Nina inquired feeling solace in Tarak's response.

Tarak appeared a little on edge then quickly said, "I'll explain it when we meet again. Until then, rest assured I will put together a plan that will lead to your victory."

With Tarak's last word still reaching Nina's ears she found herself laying on her parent's bedroom floor. Her mom was still asleep, but Nina could hear her dad downstairs making coffee. She tiptoed downstairs and asked Marc to make her a cup of hot cocoa. In an effort to brighten his daughter's morning after her rough night he topped her hot cocoa with a mountain of whipped cream. Naturally when Nina took her first sip the whipped cream got all over her mouth and nose. Marc then lead his daughter into the bathroom where she could see her adorably messy face.

They both laughed at the amusing sight. He had successfully lifted his daughter's spirits.

Together they remained at the table drinking their hot beverages talking about going to see Santa later that day. The excitement of Christmas quickly approaching distracted Nina from thinking about Amos. At least for the time being and better yet she had missed Tarak using the words "your victory" before sending her home.

Challenges Begin

After the trip to see Santa and a meal at one of Nina's favorite restaurants she was feeling a whole lot better. Finishing her pizza in record time gave her more time to play several games at the restaurant earning herself dozens of tickets. Nina struggled to keep all the tickets in her hands as she walked to the prize counter. After the cashier counted her tickets Nina was able to get a purple bracelet and a hot pink whistle with a thin matching rope. It didn't seem like much to Marc or Valerie but Nina was thrilled with her prizes. After hanging the whistle from her neck Nina gave it a good blow creating a loud shrilling noise.

By the time they arrived home Nina was feeling tired. It had been a very busy day after a long tough night, so neither of her parents were surprised when she fell asleep on the couch. They let her rest until bedtime when Marc carried her up to her room. Nina was still so exhausted she didn't wake up during the transition into her bed.

Nina's nose picked up the sweet fragrance of something baking. She stretched her arms high above her head, not realizing her hands didn't hit her headboard and extended her legs as far as they could go pointing her toes. This made her body feel so much better. Nina sat up and looked around. "Where am I?" she thought to herself. That's when she noticed the blocks she and Roo had played with.

Just then in came Roo. "Oh good, you're awake."

Roo's smiling face lifted Nina's spirits. Any apprehension she may have had disappeared. Her friend was there and Nina knew she was safe at the ranch. "Hi Roo," greeted Nina. "What smells so good?"

Roo gave Nina a warm hug saying, "Oatmeal cookies. Would you like some?"

"Yes," answered Nina rising from the floor. She didn't want to know when or why she arrived at the ranch. All Nina wanted to do was have fun with her friend.

The two enjoyed the freshly baked cookies with a cool glass of milk. Nina noticed the milk tasted different than the milk at home and asked what kind of milk it was. Roo kindly said, "It's fresh milk from yesterday morning. I made sure to milk Goldie so we'd have milk for today."

"You know how to milk a cow?" asked Nina.

"I sure do. I know how to do lots of things at the ranch," Roo replied.

"Would you teach me how to milk a cow?"

"Sure I can do that." Roo took a huge bite of a cookie and a drink of her milk before saying, "There's so much I need to teach you."

Nina didn't catch Roo's choice of words. Why would Roo "need" to teach Nina how to milk a cow and whatever else she was referring to? Nina would discover the answer to that unasked question very soon. There wasn't much time to learn how to protect Sovanna from becoming a land governed by fears, horrors and distress. Roo knew all too well how much Sovanna was relying on Nina to be brave and smart.

Goldie was appropriately named. Her hair was a light golden-brown that glistened with golden sparkles when the sun hit it just right. She had white around her eyes, nose and legs. Nervously Nina took a seat on the small stool after Roo had showed her how to milk Goldie. With some encouragement Nina reached under the cow and took hold of Goldie's teats, "Ohhhhh," squealed Goldie making Nina fall backwards off the stool.

Both Roo and Goldie were laughing hysterically. At last Goldie caught her breath and apologized, "I'm terribly sorry Nina, but it's a rite of passage around here."

"It's true," attested Roo. "Goldie did the same thing to me, a long long time ago."

Nina wasn't sure that made her feel any better, but the happy tears streaming down Roo's face did the trick. Nina soon found herself laughing along while Roo shared the story of Goldie playing the same trick on her. The more Nina laughed at Roo and eventually herself the better she felt. Nina had been so consumed by worries and fears that the jovial sparkle in her eyes was diminishing. When Nina's eyes once again danced with exuberance Roo felt it was time to move on to the hard truths Nina needed to know.

Tarak joined them in the barn and he shared a look with Roo that went unnoticed by Nina who was having a lengthy conversation with Goldie. She was thoroughly enjoying all the stories of the various pranks Goldie had played on people and other animals over the years. When Nina finally noticed Tarak she quickly thanked Goldie for sharing so many wonderful stories and turned to face him.

"Hello Tarak," Nina greeted.

Tarak bowed his head saying, "Hello my dear one."

Nina would soon learn that when Tarak added the word "my" in front of "dear one" something important was about to be said. Nina would grow to believe it was a deliberate act on Tarak's part. He didn't do anything by accident.

Roo asked Nina to have a seat on a bale of hay. As she did Nina watched Roo begin pacing back and forth across the floor. Tarak waited patiently for Roo to gather her thoughts. When she spoke, Roo sounded much more like a grown-up than a child. "Nina I'm sure you've figured out that I have been in Sovanna a long time," but before Nina could say anything Roo continued. "Goldie's little prank is one of the funny things the two of us now share," Roo paused and glanced over at Tarak whose expression conveyed bold confidence.

Nerves raced through Nina's body and she blurted out, "Just tell me!"

Tarak spoke in a calm unwavering cadence as he disclosed a hard truth, "Nina we need you to rid Sovanna of Amos and all that possesses him."

Nina rose to her feet, "And how am I supposed to do that?"

Roo took Nina's hands in hers and together they sat down in the hay. "I realize how scary that sounds Nina..."

Nina interrupted her angrily, "Do you? How could you know? And stop talking to me like you're my mom!"

"I'm sorry Nina. Please let me explain." Roo's intensely concerned eyes let Nina know she needed to listen. "When I first arrived in Sovanna I had nothing but fun like you, but also like you I was soon faced with my fears. My fears were in a different animal form because I had different fears than you do."

"What kind of animal did you have?"

"That doesn't matter Nina. What matters is I had to conquer each one of my biggest fears and when I did my fear animal disappeared into nothingness. Sovanna was safe from all my fears and it's been a gloriously dreamy place ever since."

"So no bad things ever happen?"

Roo smiled a warm loving smile, "No. Nothing but good and marvelous things happen here."

"Until I came here," moaned a sorrowful Nina with her head hanging low.

Hugging Nina tightly Roo said, "Remember the same thing happened when I came here. It's part of the process. We both want to enjoy the kindhearted play of childhood innocence. However, children have fears and those fears would rather force us to have hurtful, appalling encounters with beastly forces."

Sarcastically Nina replied with terror in her voice, "Oh sure, I'll just go out there and make Amos go away."

"Nina, I understand this seems like a daunting task. One that you couldn't possibly do, but you wouldn't have been brought here if you didn't have the skills needed to defeat Amos."

That gave Nina a way out or so she thought. "Yes you brought me here so just send me home and don't ever bring me back. That way Amos goes away."

"If it were only that simple," groaned Roo.

Tarak spoke in a calm soothing manner, "You carry your fears with you wherever you go dear one. You may not be aware of them, but you know they can rear their ugly heads at any moment. When we first brought you here we knew you would eventually have to face your fears. What we didn't know was how quickly Amos would make his presence known. Even if you never came back Amos would surely take over Sovanna. That's the sole reason he is here and now that he's arrived he is here to stay. He has one desire. To fill this place with every fear known to man and he will start by spreading your fears into all that reside here. Then he will capitalize on our individual fears until Sovanna becomes one continuous nightmare. The cold hard truth is you and only you my dear one can vanquish him."

Tears flowed freely from Nina's eyes and she whimpered, "I don't know how to make him go away. I'm afraid of him. I don't want to see him again and really don't want to go anywhere with him. I know it won't be anywhere good," Nina struggled to speak before finally saying in between sobs, "How do I fight him?"

Roo looked Nina square in the eyes and with tenderness said, "I wish I could tell you Nina, but that is something you have to discover for yourself. Your fears can't be overcome by me or even Tarak, they must be subdued in a way that only you would think of."

"You guys keep using words I don't understand," shouted Nina feeling overwhelmed by her situation and the way everyone spoke in Sovanna.

"I'm sorry. Basically, you need to find a way to not be afraid of your deepest fears and that will make each fear go away one at a time which will cause Amos to disappear," explained Roo in the simplest way she could.

"How did you do it?" pleaded an earnest Nina.

"I don't remember. Once my fears were banished, which means forced to leave Sovanna," Roo clarified, "I forgot what I used to be afraid of and how I made them go away."

"That doesn't help me," cried Nina who then said something she never thought she would, "It would have been better if I never came here."

Kumah jumped onto Nina's lap trying to break her spiral of despair. Kumah looked up at Nina with her dark brown eyes and confidently said, "Nina you have one of the greatest imaginations I've ever seen. I believe your creativity is boundless and with that I know you will imagine your way out of any fearful situation. Trust your playful and clever imagination to help you."

"I concur. My dear one, you're very talented in the world of make-believe. I trust you will find new and gifted ways to use your imaginative play to keep you from harm," assured Tarak, "Besides once you have rid Sovanna of Amos there is something even more wonderful waiting for you."

Before Nina could respond she found herself on a wooden dinghy surrounded by angry waves. There wasn't any land to be seen and not only didn't the boat have oars or a motor it was also leaking. Nina couldn't swim and her fear of drowning came to the forefront. Screaming for help until her voice gave out proved to be a waste of time. The small boat was more than halfway submerged making Nina shiver in the icy water. Her fear of drowning gripped her like never before. All she wanted to do was go home and never again use Great-Grandma's music box. Gram's voice echoed around Nina from every direction. She said, "Nina, pretend we're playing in my house. You're on my couch not in a boat, you see the waves coming to take you under. What would you pretend?"

With her eyes closed she imagined she was safely playing at Gram's house. She pictured the threatening waves rising higher around her, but instead of being afraid of drowning an idea came to her. Nina jumped from the boat into the water. Laughter escaped her lips as she thought, "Mermaids don't drown. I can breathe in the water and out of the water. I'm a magical mermaid." That's when Nina opened her eyes. She was under the water with an array of colorful fishes swimming all around her. Her tail glistened in the rays of sunlight coming through the water's surface. She marveled at its beautiful greenish-blue color that shimmered and gleamed with every move of her tail. The golden-bronze accents around her waist and at the ends of her tailfin were almost blinding bright when the sun hit them directly. A matching tube top was wrapped around Nina's upper body completing her ensemble.

Nina was so excited to be a mermaid. She swam as fast as she could in a deep dive then in one fluid motion she headed for the surface. She broke through the water and soared high into the air before flipping over and diving back into the water. Nina swam around a coral reef for a while, then she moved on to a sunken ship where she found a mirror to admire her new look. Her dark hair went halfway down her tail and was kept off her face by a beaded headband made from white Nassa shells. As Nina came out of the sunken ship she spotted dolphins swimming by. Nina rushed to join them and swam alongside the pod until they spotted an island. A young dolphin followed Nina toward the island until it's mother summoned it back to her.

Nina waved goodbye to the calf and swam to the shore. Sitting in the waist deep water Nina soaked in the beauty around her. She could hardly believe she was actually a mermaid making her shout at the top of her lungs, "I'm a mermaid!" She couldn't help but laugh at her remarkable transformation. As Nina continued to laugh she felt her fear of water and drowning lift from her. At that exact moment, she spotted Amos dragging himself through the sand. The dolphins were still in sight and Nina felt secure in her ability to swim away from him, but something made her stay. Amos looked a bit smaller than she remembered and he was definitely in pain. When his dreary eyes made eye contact with her Nina was transported back to the ranch.

Roo squeezed Nina until it was hard for her to breath causing Nina to ask Roo to let her go. Kumah bounced up and down in front of Nina making happy little squeaks. She was talking so fast Nina couldn't understand what she was saying. Then there was Tarak who proudly nodded at Nina before saying, "I'm so very proud of you dear one. Your courage and quick thinking has wiped away your first fear. I knew you would be successful."

Before she could say a word Nina's excitement over beating Amos and the thrill of being a mermaid faded. It was quickly replaced by pure and utter fatigue. Her body took control and she began to wobble on her feet. Before she hit the floor of the barn Gram's music box returned her safely to her bed.

A Welcomed Hiatus

Days went by without anything magical happening and if Nina were honest she welcomed the break. Her time as a mermaid would remain one of her most treasured memories and she could clearly recall every single detail, but there was one thing that still concerned her. Conquering her fear in Sovanna did little to change her fear of water in the real world. She still didn't know how to swim and becoming a mermaid outside the magical realm was an impossibility.

A couple days later during dinner Nina posed a question, "Can I take swimming lessons?"

Valerie and Marc briefly looked at each other before replying. Nina's mom asked, "You want to learn how to swim during Christmas break?"

"No, it's too cold now, but in the summer. One of my friends at school learned how to swim last summer." Which answered Valerie's next question.

"I'm sure we can make that happen," Marc replied.

Valerie agreed adding, "I'll start looking for swim instructors after the holidays. That'll give us time to find one we think would be a good fit for you." She wasn't sure what prompted her daughter to want to learn to swim but Valerie was relieved she did. They knew several people with pools and visiting them meant being on high alert especially if they were outside by the pool. Nina's parents had enrolled Nina in swimming classes at a local park years back, but between her almost frantic apprehension about the water and a full class with a new instructor things didn't go well. As a matter-of-fact Nina's parents believed it only intensified her trepidation.

Nina smiled. Learning to swim would help take away her fear of drowning and although it wouldn't be as much fun as being a mermaid, by any stretch of her imagination, she felt good about her decision. Overcoming her fear of drowning in Sovanna had given her the confidence to do the same at home.

When the doorbell rang shortly after dinner Nina remembered Grandma was staying with them through the New Year. Theresa's arrival meant Christmas was just around the corner. Nina rushed into Theresa's arms saying, "Grandma you're here." Nina loved it when Grandma spent the night. Theresa would sleep in Nina's room and say she felt like a princess sleeping in Nina's canopy bed. The sheer peach fabric draping from the tester and cinched up on the columnar posts did resemble a princess's bed. However, it was Grandma's amusement and appreciation for Nina's bed that caused her to remember how excited she was the first-time Grandma slept in her room. That was the main reason Grandma bought a canopy bed for Nina's room in her condo. She wanted Nina to feel like a princess when she visited.

Theresa read her granddaughter a story, kissed her cheek and said goodnight then quickly feel asleep. Nina on the other hand tossed and turned with Christmas excitement bubbling in her belly. She wondered what items on her Christmas list would actually be under the tree. At last she slumbered and her dreams picked up where her wondering left off. Joyous dreams had begun filling her night's several days earlier and continued through Christmas Eve.

Nina's eyes popped open even before the sun rose. Impatiently she quietly laid on her side staring at her window waiting for any sign of daylight. What felt like an eternity went by until at long last the first sunbeam shone through the corner of her window. Nina popped up in bed saying, "It's Christmas!" That's when she noticed Grandma wasn't in bed. Leaping from her bed Nina ran to her parent's room still yelling, "It's Christmas! It's Christmas!" Neither of her parents were in their room or bathroom so Nina ran towards the stairs.

"It's Christmas!!! Can I come down?" inquired Nina knowing she couldn't go downstairs on Christmas morning until she was invited to come down.

There was no answer at first making Nina's heart skip a beat.

Was something wrong? Then she heard her dad say, "You can come down now."

Marc was recording Nina's descent catching her wide-eye expression at the sight of all the presents under and around the tree. Mom and Grandma were sitting on the couch smiling with affection as Nina approached. "Merry Christmas," greeted Valerie giving Nina a longer than normal hug. Both Marc and Theresa followed suit and then the gift giving began.

After tearing open countless presents Nina remembered she had gifts to hand out. Nina handed all three of her wrapped treasures to their recipients and waited with bated breath. Marc said, "Ladies first," followed by Nina repeating his words.

Mom went first after complimenting Nina on her wrapping skills. It took some doing with the amount of tape securing the wrinkled and bunched wrapping paper, but in the end Valerie uncovered the box. Nina was thankful the picture of the angel was facing away from her mom. Valerie opened the box and with deliberate movements separated the tissue paper from its contents. "Oh my goodness, it's beautiful Nina." Looking at her daughter she continued, "I love it bumblebee, thank you so much and I know exactly where I'm going to put it." Valerie rose to her feet, walked over to the TV hutch and placed her angel figurine front and center on the top shelf. Nina ran into her mom's waiting arms thrilled that her mom liked her present.

"I guess I'm next," Theresa remarked. Smiling through all the work it took to free her present from its cocoon-like wrapping. Grandma's face lit up when she saw the front of her coffee cup, "It's perfect jellybean. Thank you for getting me a new coffee cup. I needed one and this is my new favorite," Theresa exclaimed hugging Nina.

"Your turn Dad," urged Nina excited to see his reaction.

Marc was able to open his present much quicker and when he saw what was written on the street sign he said, "Thank you angel, it's going to look great out by my barbecue." Marc gave Nina a big hug, placed the sign on the end table and said, "I think you have a few more to open Nina."

"That's true, you do," agreed Valerie sharing a covert wink with her husband.

Nina knew Santa's gifts were the last ones to open and they were usually items her parents would say were too expensive for them to buy for her. "Thank goodness for Santa," Nina thought to herself. It wasn't that she didn't appreciate all the other presents, but Santa's were always extra special, in part because he came from the North Pole to give her things on her Christmas wish list. Sure enough Santa had done it again. Nina received a princess tent that matched her bed filled with new stuffed animals, a scooter and doll house complete with furnishings, people and pets. "Thank you Santa!" shouted Nina into the sky.

"Wow! You must have been a very good girl this year for Santa to bring you all that," said Theresa.

"I was," Nina confirmed with humility in her voice as she began playing with the doll house.

"Wait Nina, I found another present behind the tree with your name on it," her dad said.

"I wonder what that could be?" Valerie teased.

"Who is it from?" blurted Nina eyeing the small square present in her dad's hand. She had already opened the presents from her family and Santa. Part of her wondered if it was from someone in Sovanna.

"It says from Mom and Dad on the tag," replied Marc.

Nina took the small package saying, "I thought I opened all your gifts."

"I guess we missed this one," shrugged Marc. Valerie was now filled with anticipation and finding it hard to sit still. Marc gave her a loving look helping to soothe her building excitement.

Nina tore open the wrapping paper tossing it to the floor. She was unable to open the square gray box due to the sides being taped. "I need help," she said handing it to her dad. Marc cut through the tape with his pocket knife and handed the box back to Nina. Before Nina could open it, her mom told her to be very careful.

Nina removed the lid of the box and found sparkly tissue paper hiding whatever was inside. Nina sat the box on the couch and pulled the tissue paper opened. Nestled in the box was a shimmering white round Christmas ornament with a cartoonish girl with raised hands and a big smile on it. There were little pink flowers arched over the words above the drawing of the girl. Nina tried to sound them out, "I'm being pro...mo.." she looked up at her mom and said, "What's that word?"

"Promoted," answered Valerie. "It means you're getting to be something you weren't before. Let me help you read it." Nina handed the ornament still in the box over to her mom and Valerie said, "Let's read it together."

Nina wasn't sure she needed any more help but together they slowly read, "I'm being promoted to a big sister." Nina's eyes widened and she looked at each of her parents before inquiring, "I'm going to have a baby sister or brother?"

"Yes you are," replied a blissful Valerie.

Marc and Valerie enveloped Nina in their arms before Valerie asked, "What do you think of having a brother or sister?"

"I think it's great!" answered Nina before asking to hang her big sister ornament on the tree. "I'll have someone to play and have fun with," she continued as she smiled at her final Christmas gift hanging on the tree.

By Christmas evening Nina had played with the majority of her presents keeping her busy throughout the day. The only time she stopped playing was to eat and it was during lunch when she noticed her mom sleeping on the couch. Curiosity got the best of Nina and she asked, "Is mom sleeping so much because of the baby?"

"Yes angel," Marc replied, "But she won't always be this tired, she'll start feeling better soon."

The family watched a Christmas movie after eating dinner, but Nina fell asleep on the floor halfway through. Exhausted from waking up before dawn and a full day of imaginative play caused Nina to sleep much later than normal the following morning. When she finally made her way downstairs she discovered everyone had already eaten and were busy cleaning up the mess from Christmas. Dad soon took her princess tent upstairs persuading Nina to quickly finish her breakfast. Once done she went upstairs to play with her new toys. Marc made a few more trips up and down the stairs bringing up the rest of her gifts. Nina struggled trying to decide what to play with first. Upon Marc's final trip he told her to find a spot for all her new toys and then they could go outside and hang his barbecue sign before the rain hit.

Nina looked around her room feeling a bit overwhelmed at all she had to put away, not to mention being sad she couldn't just start playing, but she wanted to watch her dad hang his gift so she began her work. "We can help," announced a shrill voice from inside the princess tent. When Nina turned around she saw all the stuffed animals standing in the entrance of the tent. Front and center was a small white lamb, "Would you like us to help?" asked the lamb in the same high-pitched voice.

"That would be great," expressed Nina with a huge smile.

Together Nina and her new friends made quick work of putting things away. A bright green parrot with red and yellow wings was especially helpful flying around and directing the other stuffed animals on where things should go. Crackers, was the name the parrot had given Nina when he introduced himself and his name fit him to a tee. He couldn't stop talking about his favorite crackers in between squawking his instructions. When all the work was done, Crackers landed on Nina's arm and asked, "Do you have any crackers?"

Nina didn't, but that didn't stop her. She imagined there were crackers inside her small pink tin usually filled with bracelets. With eager anticipation Nina slowly opened the tin to find it was filled with little square crackers. She fed Crackers so many she was sure he would pop open his stitching. Thankfully he remained unharmed after gorging himself on the entire contents of the little tin box. Nina was having so much fun laughing and talking with Crackers that she failed to notice all the other toys had returned to the tent and were no longer alive.

Looking around her room Nina was pleased with the results and headed downstairs with Crackers in her arms. "I'm ready Dad," she proudly announced.

"You're sure everything is put away?" Marc questioned wanting confirmation.

"Yep," answered Nina with a giggle. "Cracker and the other animals helped me."

Amused by his daughter's response and impressed by her already finding a name for one of her new toys he asked, "Crackers? How'd you come up with that name?"

"Because he really really likes crackers," Nina replied in a matter-of-fact way.

"Well that sounds very logical for a parrot," agreed Marc before heading outside to hang his street sign. Nina smiled with pride when Dad was done securing the sign onto the wooden fence. The sign looked great and Marc had finished just in time as the first sprinkles of rain landed on their heads.

It had been an amazing Christmas for the entire family making Nina forget she still had battles to win in Sovanna. How she hoped those could wait. Nina didn't feel ready to face another fear, she wasn't sure she would ever be ready, but something deep inside her chest told her she didn't have a choice. Thankfully that feeling quickly faded allowing Nina to enjoy the simple pleasures of life at home. Unfortunately, Nina was on borrowed time.

Warnings and Accolades

A couple days later Marc took Valerie to a doctor's appointment leaving Nina with her grandma. Theresa found Nina staring at her big sister Christmas ornament. She watched Nina for several minutes before asking, "What do you think about being a big sister?"

Nina turned and faced her grandma then with a beaming smile said, "I can't wait, it's going to be so much fun."

"It is going to be fun not only for you but for all of us. This baby will be my second grandbaby which is quite something."

Nina hadn't thought about the baby being anything more than a new brother or sister for her. "That's true," was all she could think to say and when she noticed tears welling in Grandma's eyes Nina wondered why she would be crying about the baby. "Are you sad about the baby?" questioned Nina confused by Theresa's behavior.

Grandma motioned for Nina to come to her saying, "No jellybean, these are happy tears."

"Happy tears?" Nina had never heard of someone crying because they were happy. The only time she cried was when she was scared or hurt.

"Yes, happy tears are when something you've been hoping for finally comes true making it extra wonderful. This is the first-time in generations that a second child was born into the family. Your mom is an only child; I am an only child and your great-grandma was also an only child. None of us had a brother or sister."

This was new information. Nina had never looked passed the fact that she was an only child and that only stood out to her because her friends at school all had siblings. "Why?" she asked, wondering why there were so many only children in her family.

"It just happened that way. I know I wanted more children and I believe my mom did as well but neither of us ever had any more. Your mom and dad have been waiting a long time to give you a baby brother or sister and at last it's happening."

Theresa paused then posed the question, "Do you want a baby sister or a baby brother?"

Nina considered the question for several moments before answering. "Do I get to pick?"

Theresa laughed at her question, "No jellybean. I was just wondering if one sounded better than the other."

"Nope, they sound the same," blurted Nina, but then thoughts rushed to her mind and she continued, "If it's a sister we can share my toys and play dress up, but if it's a boy he might not want to play what I want to play. That wouldn't be fun if we couldn't play together." Her words were honest and Nina wasn't trying to be mean, she was simply speaking from her heart.

"Those are good points, but having a brother doesn't mean he wouldn't play with you. I believe whatever the baby is you two will have all kinds of fun. Perhaps a baby brother may think of new things to play that you've never thought of. Boys can be lots of fun to play with too jellybean. Do you like playing with your dad?"

"Yes. Dad's do lots of things Mom's don't do." That's when Nina remembered one special day with Marc. "One time a pipe broke in the backyard and there were puddles all over the grass. Dad had to dig up the grass to fix it. He let me help and I got all muddy and wet so I made mud pies with my hands. It was so much fun," giggled Nina.

Theresa chuckled at the memory of seeing pictures of Nina soaking wet and playing in the mud as Marc repaired the broken sprinkler pipe. "I remember that story. You must have needed a bath when your dad was done."

"I did. I even made mud in the tub," boasted Nina.

"So how did you get clean?"

"Mom let the water out and I took a second bath with clean water."

"So you agree, boys can be lots of fun too," Theresa pointed out adding, "With your imagination I'm sure you'll find all kinds of things to do with the baby. It truly doesn't matter if it's a boy or a girl."

"Especially with the music box. We can go on all kinds of adventures," Nina said jumping up and down at the mere thought. It would be such a wonderful treat to share her magical adventures with someone, especially a sibling. Nina's anticipation bubbled over as she spun in circles repeatedly shouting, "I'm going to be a big sister!"

Theresa laughed at her granddaughter's exuberance then asked, "Are you having fun with the piano?"

"Yes. Do you want to go play?" Nina implored. She knew it would be like playing with her mom, but part of the fun was watching all the toys come to life with Valerie being none the wiser. Nina grabbed Cracker, her new favorite toy, and said, "Come on it'll be fun."

No sooner did Grandma begin winding the music box did Cracker start talking Nina's ear off. For old time's sake Theresa said, "Play me a tale," and unbeknownst to Theresa the toys in Nina's room began yelling, "It's playtime!"

Grandma did an amazing job trying to pretend she could hear Cracker talking, but all the magical activities going on around her went unseen. Perhaps Theresa felt she was missing out on what once was or it was something else, but whatever the reason Grandma asked, "How about we play hide and seek?"

"Okay," agreed Nina.

"We have to stay upstairs and play," instructed Theresa.

Theresa hid first and Nina found her within a minute standing behind her parent's bathroom door. Grandma didn't seem to be too good at hiding so Nina figured she'd try and help by showing her some of her best hiding places. First she hid in the empty clothes hamper, next behind her dad's heavy winter coats hanging in his closet and finally in one of the leftover boxes from Christmas that had been put aside for donations. Christmas time always meant getting rid of clothes that no longer fit and toys that weren't being played with.

Grandma wasn't catching on so Nina suggested something that popped into her head as the music box song reached her ears, "You could pretend you're a chair or a blanket or something like that. Then I would have a much harder time finding you." Nina knew the magic wouldn't work for Grandma, but perhaps because Nina was playing with Grandma there was a slim chance the magic would allow it.

Suddenly Theresa was frozen in place with her mouth half open as she was beginning to speak. Kumah was jumping on the floor near Nina's feet with fear in her eyes. As loudly as her little voice could she shouted, "Oh no, that's too dangerous! Nina, you can never turn yourself into an inanimate object or anyone else for that matter."

"Why is it dangerous?"

Nina picked Kumah up in her hand and let her explain, "When Theresa was little and was playing with the music box she played hide and seek with her toys. It was a lot of fun and she thought the same thing you did. If she turned herself into a pillow her toys would have a really hard time finding her and they did."

Nina interrupted, "So it worked," confirmed Nina who wasn't sure why hiding so well could be dangerous.

"It worked too well. As a pillow, she couldn't move or talk. She just laid on her bed screaming in her head for help as all her toys searched for her."

"Why couldn't she move or talk?" asked a puzzled Nina.

"Because pillows, chairs and things that aren't alive strip you of those abilities. All she could do was what a pillow normally does, just lay there."

With a serious tone Nina said, "That's scary."

"It was very scary for your grandma. She thought she would be a pillow for the rest of her life."

"What happened?"

"Your Great-Grandma Ruth came into the room and looked for her, but when she couldn't find her she picked up the piano and said, 'Light up my daughter,' and with that Theresa started to glow. When Grams noticed the glowing pillow on her daughter's bed she walked over to it, picked it up and held it in her arms saying, 'Bring Theresa back to me please,' and poof she turned back into herself and she gave her mom the biggest hug ever."

"That was close," replied Nina.

Kumah stressed to Nina how important it was to never pretend to be an inanimate object, which she had to explain in simpler terms. Kumah continued to emphasize how important it was for Nina to always remember to keep that rule. Making it abundantly clear didn't seem to do the job as Nina casually crossed her heart and promised never to pretend to be something that wasn't alive. Her half-hearted promise wasn't enough.

Nina's mind wondered while Kumah warned her over and over how careful she needed to be when playing with the music box and to never ever break her promise. When Kumah finally stopped talking Nina asked, "How did Grams know how to save Grandma?"

"Your great-grandma never stopped believing in the magic of the music box. It was a lot of fun because together they would have the best playtime."

Nina considered Kumah's answer. "So the only reason Grams was able to save Grandma was because she still believed in magic?"

"Yes. By believing she knew what question to ask to find Theresa and what to ask for to change her from a pillow back into herself. If your Grams had stopped believing in magic I don't know what would have happened."

That answer convinced Nina that no matter what happened, she would never turn into something that was lifeless. Neither Grandma or Mom believed in magic so if Nina made the same mistake her grandmother did it would be very bad. Without someone believing in the piano's power Nina could find herself spending the rest of her life frozen as a lifeless object. Nina vowed to never make that mistake. Her more sincere vow made Kumah vanish in her hand and Grandma unfreeze.

"We're home," announced Marc.

Grandma and Nina rushed downstairs and were thrilled that they had brought lunch. Hamburgers and fries from a local diner hit the spot. During their meal Valerie told them the baby was doing well and growing as expected. It was the first-time Valerie came close to finishing a meal in months. Marc was the first to notice and happily commented, "It looks like you're getting your appetite back." With a mouthful of food Valerie nodded in agreement.

Nina found herself bored from the adult conversation so after asking to be excused she headed upstairs to play with her new toys. Crackers greeted her and that's when Nina noticed the piano was playing its song. Crackers gave a loud squawk before flying off. A cold wind made Nina shiver despite the beaming sunlight coming through her closed window. She spun around searching for the source of the wind and found herself in Sovanna. Tarak stood on top of a hill in the distance and when they made eye contact, even with the large separation between them, Nina could see an intensity in his eyes. The magnitude of his confident reassuring stare would stick with her throughout the next harrowing experience.

What happened next reminded Nina of the dimming lamp on her nightstand. When Nina was younger her mom would dim the lamp into a soft subtle night light, but now that same thing was happening outside in the middle of the day. Tarak and the rolling hills surrounding Nina became darker and darker until she was surrounded by a sunless void. No matter which way she looked there was nothing but pure darkness. Nina lifted her hand in front of her face but she couldn't see it. Even moving her hand closer until she could feel her nose didn't help. Nina wouldn't have believed this level of total unwavering blackness was possible, but here she was in the midst of it. She didn't like the dark and this degree of nothingness surrounding her was terrifying. Even with her skilled imagination Nina couldn't have dreamt up such darkness.

As if being swallowed up by this desolate and threatening place wasn't enough, Nina could hear the chilling sound of whimpering far off in the distance. As the whimpering drew closer she started hearing screams, growling and moans. Nina closed her eyes while doing her best to pull her limbs in tightly to her body trying to shrink in size. Petrified in place Nina couldn't move a muscle, then the look of strength in Tarak's eyes came to mind and Nina took a deep breath. "Think Nina, think," she ordered to herself.

Her first thought was to become a flashlight, but that wouldn't work she'd be forever stuck as a flashlight. "Come on Nina use your imagination," she muttered under her breath. As the frightening noises around her continued to get closer she wished she could fly away, but in the absolute darkness she didn't know if it was safe to do so; however, thinking about getting her feet off the ground helped her to remember her tennis shoes. Her white shoes were covered with little gold stars giving her an ingenious idea.

Nina started stomping her feet as hard as she could while ordering the stars to take to the sky. With each stomp, more and more stars flew from her shoes into what had been a starless mass of black. As the stars filled every inch of the darkness Nina could sense light through her still closed eyes. Slowly she opened one eye then the other. Nina was fascinated by the sight before her and soon found herself giggling as the star's bound from her shoes into the sky. Eventually the size of the dark spots still in the sky became minimal.

Gazing up at the illuminated brilliance surrounding her made her laugh loud and hard. Then Nina switched up her stomping to more of a dance never wavering in her determination to completely fill the sky with stars. Each and every star made the darkness give way to an increasingly stunning sight. As the sky filled with more and more stars something new occurred. Colorful clouds ranging from grays to yellowish-orange lined the horizon. Suddenly a beacon of light shot from high above, resembling a lighthouse. The brilliant beam of light chased away any remaining hint of darkness. A radiant glow unlike anything Nina had ever experienced now surrounded her. It was as if the light was hugging her and filling her with sense of security. The infinite darkness that had held Nina captive was no more.

Tarak raced full speed towards Nina and upon reaching her he carefully laid his forehead against hers making sure not to bump her with his massive antlers. Nina threw her arms around Tarak's neck as far as they could reach and they remained in silence until they heard a weak voice. Amos laid on his side near Nina's feet and in between his labored breaths whispered, "I'll be back," he warned. Nina had the perfect response, in a quickened pace she stomped her feet shooting stars from her shoes all over him. In no time, he was completely covered in glistening golden stars. Seconds later the stars returned to Nina's shoes and Amos was gone.

"You are so courageous dear one and your creative intelligence makes you more than a worthy adversary. I have no doubt you will rid Sovanna of Amos regardless of what he tries next time."

Nina knew Tarak was doing his best to comfort her, but the words "next time" did nothing more than remind her she would have to face another one of her fears. Being victorious the last two times helped her feel a little better, but how much more of this could she take? How many more fears would she have to conquer to rid Sovanna of Amos?

Family Time

As the night crept towards midnight Nina grew more and more excited. However, her excitement was beginning to lose out to fatigue. Knowing their daughter wouldn't make it until midnight Marc had recorded a New Year's Eve countdown from a different time zone. Valerie distracted Nina with New Year's Eve surprises while Marc prepared the VHS recording. First Valerie placed a sparkly tiara on Nina's head. It was covered in egg-shaped rhinestones, with the words "Happy New Year" written out in shimmering magenta spheres. The cluster of large red and blue oval rhinestones at the center peak of the little crown resembled a flower adding the final touch to the tiara. Nina then had to pick from the matching necklaces. They were lined with shining translucent beads with a large circle at the end that said "Happy New Year." Nina had a hard time deciding which was her favorite. She looked over the purple, gold, silver, red and blue chains before declaring, "I think the red and blue are my favorites because they match my crown. Even the shape of the beads is the same as my crown."

"It's almost time," announced Marc after pushing the play button on the remote.

An excited Nina watched people dance along to a song that a flamboyant band played. The lead singer dressed in a black suit and blue neon shirt jumped and spun around the stage while he sang. Valerie commented that he was going to fall off the stage if he wasn't careful. Nina didn't even hear her mom's comment; she was too busy watching all the people dance with their various hats, crowns and glasses all saying "Happy New Year" on them. Nina spotted a lady wearing a very similar tiara and shouted, "Look she has a crown like me!"

"It does look like yours," agreed Grandma who was the only one sitting on the couch. She had caught a cold and was doing her best to keep the cold medicine from making her fall asleep.

After the band played a couple more songs the announcer said, "We're only a minute away from the new year," filling Nina with anticipation.

The next thing Nina saw was a huge glittering ball high on top of a building. Below the ball was the number 60 which soon changed to 59, 58, 57 and so on. The countdown to a new year had begun. When the number 10 flashed the massive crowd in the streets below started the countdown. Nina and her parents joined in and after shouting the number one Nina realized her parents had grown quiet. She looked over at them and found them sharing a kiss before turning towards her and saying, "Happy New Year Nina."

"Happy New Year!" Nina cheered rushing to hug her parents. Next came Nina's favorite way of celebrating the new year. She got to blow bubbles in the house filling the living room with floating globes of air that popped as soon as they made contact with anything. This was the one time of the year she could get away with blowing bubbles indoors, but not for lack of trying.

After all the fun Nina headed up to bed feeling thankful that she still had the weekend before having to go back to school. It had been the most marvelous holiday break she could remember. Between finding out she was going to have a baby brother or sister, Grandma staying through the New Year and all her Christmas gifts Nina could hardly contain her joy. The only thing that put a damper on her happiness was Grandma choosing to sleep on the couch in hopes Nina wouldn't catch her cold.

Although it wasn't actually close to midnight Nina felt drained. Slumber came moments after her parents had tucked her in. Without so much as rolling over Nina awoke in the same position she had fallen asleep in. That was highly unusual for her. There was a very good reason she had a full-size bed, it was a deliberate act on her parent's part. When Nina was in her crib she would turn and twist in every direction. The only reason she didn't end up on the floor was because of the railing, so when it came time for her to move to a big girl bed Valerie knew a twin would end badly. Nina was far too much of a spirited sleeper and her mom knew a twin bed would mean lots of tumbles onto the floor.

There was however one morning several years back when Valerie and Marc had quite the scare. Valerie had gone in to wake Nina but she couldn't find her. Valerie checked the floor, under the bed and still no Nina. Panic pulsed through her veins as she called for Marc. Together they checked the windows and doors, everything was still locked and secure. After checking throughout the house and calling out for their daughter they rushed back into her room for one final search before calling the authorities.

"Nina, Nina," lamented Valerie with tears overwhelming her eyes.

That's when Marc noticed the pile of blankets at the foot of Nina's bed begin to shift. As the movement became more obvious Marc rushed to the mound of tangled bed linens where he uncovered a drowsy Nina. Valerie wrapped her sleepy daughter in her arms and let the tears stream down her cheeks. The fearful tears that were burning Valerie's eyes as she fought against them were now being released as tears of utter relief.

The sunlight hit Nina's face forcing her to roll over in bed enjoying a long stretch before sitting up. The house was quiet but the sun was shining so brightly she knew it was morning. Cracker sat on her nightstand without saying or doing anything. Nina wasn't ready to revisit Sovanna knowing Amos would be waiting for her, but she did miss her new friend Cracker. In an effort to encourage him to play Nina picked him up, gave him a hug and said, "Good morning Cracker would you like to play?"

He didn't make a sound. Nina pretended he was alive and played with him for several minutes before giving up. Was something wrong with the piano's magic? Had Amos done something to Sovanna? Nina didn't know the answers to those questions and although her curiosity continued to grow there was a part of her that was okay with the magic not working. Then a horrible thought came to her mind. Had she stopped believing in magic?

Grandma was still asleep on the couch when Nina went downstairs. Valerie placed her index finger over her lips encouraging Nina to be quiet. As the two of them ate their cereal they whispered throughout their meal. Nina thought it was quite fun to do so. Grandma woke up just as they were finishing. When she wished them all a good morning she sounded worse than the day before. Still whispering Nina said, "Grandma's voice is weird." Valerie nodded in agreement and grabbed Theresa a bag of throat lozenges from the top shelf of a kitchen cabinet.

After freshening up Grandma put a lozenge in her mouth and went back to the couch. Familiar with the routine Valerie handed Theresa a pad of paper and pencil. Nina asked what that was for and her mom explained. Theresa would write down what she needed when she wanted something instead of hurting her throat by trying to speak. After a little help from Valerie and some creative coloring Nina handed her Grandma a note. It said, "I hope you feel better soon," it had pictures of flowers and birds flying in a blue sky with a bright yellow sun. Theresa drew a heart on the back of the note and blew Nina a kiss.

Marc persuaded Valerie to take Nina to do some baby shopping. He would look after Theresa and it gave his wife and daughter some alone time away from Grandma's cold. The last thing he wanted was for Valerie to get sick. She had just gotten over her morning sickness. In no time, they were ready and headed off for a fun day of shopping.

The first store they went to was rather boring as far as Nina was concerned. It was filled with car seats, high chairs, cribs and other uninteresting essentials. Nevertheless, Nina was excited to voice her opinion, but Valerie and Marc had already made their selections. Basically, they were there to buy what had already been decided on. Nina wasn't very happy about coming along, but there was a method to Valerie's madness. Getting this store out of the way first left them with all the undecided items to purchase. Valerie hid her smirk from Nina as she watched her daughter's glum expression become drearier.

Little did she know the fun was about to begin. Nina held tight to Valerie's hand as she dawdled towards the second store without looking where she was going. "Let's grab a cart Nina," announced Valerie which brought Nina's face up. That's when she noticed giant-sized baby photo's high on the walls advertising various baby items.

Scanning the store Nina noticed baby clothes, toys and so much more. Her mood quickly improved as she followed her mom towards the toy section. Of course, a newborn couldn't play with toys but that didn't mean they couldn't get the baby something to play with as it grew or just to decorate the room. Valerie stopped before reaching the toy section and asked, "What kind of theme should we have for the baby's room?"

Nina knew about birthday theme's; she would pick a different theme for each of her birthday's, but she had no idea what a good baby room theme would be. Mom to the rescue, "Let's walk through the bedding section first and decide on a theme." Nina agreed and followed Valerie down the first aisle. There were so many different designs making Nina think she wouldn't be able to decide, but it quickly occurred to her all the primarily blue or pink themes wouldn't work. She didn't know if it was a brother or a sister on their way. Eliminating all the specifically boy or girl ideas helped Nina not feel so helpless. Focusing her eyes on neutral colors was a big help and before long she spotted a bedding set she really liked. "Mom!" squealed Nina, "I like this one so much."

"Oh I think that's a beautiful choice bumblebee," agreed Valerie. The bedding was covered with characters from some of Nina's favorite fairy tale books. The colors ranged from green, yellow, purple and red to soft tones of blue and pink scattered about. Nina thought to herself pigs are supposed to be pink and the big clock with the mouse wasn't all blue. "You can always take your story books into the nursery and read to the baby while pointing out the characters in the room." Valerie's suggestion made Nina's face light up with pride and anticipation.

After the cart was filled with the matching sheets, towels swaddling blankets and anything else that matched the theme Nina was reenergized. Next they picked out wall art, stuffed animals and various baby toys with the same theme. With each new item Nina grew more excited about having a baby sister or brother. Before long the cart was nearly overflowing, but there were other necessary items to buy. Diapers, baby bottles and clothing. Much to Nina's disappointment the diapers and bottles didn't have themes, but when they went into the clothing section she discovered there were some fairy tale themed clothes. The tiny size of the clothing made it hard to believe a person could be so small. The newborn clothes were so adorable Nina was soon selecting more than they needed. Valerie finally had to say they had enough as Nina continued to find more she liked. Nina offered to carry some of the items if they wouldn't fit into the cart. Valerie clarified, "It's not that Nina, babies grow fast and I don't want to buy more than we need."

As the cashier rang up the order she noticed Nina's beaming smile and asked, "Did you help your mom pick out all this baby stuff?"

A proud Nina answered, "I did. I'm going to be a big help when the baby gets here."

"I'm sure you will," replied the elderly woman with a wink.

As they walked to the car Valerie asked Nina where she would like to go for lunch. Without hesitation Nina picked a fast food restaurant with a playground. It wasn't at all what Valerie felt like eating, but Nina had been such a trooper during their lengthy shopping day she agreed. While Nina gobbled down her lunch Valerie nibbled at her less than appetizing meal and waited until Nina went to play on the playground before pulling a snack bag from her purse. She had begun carrying it when she was dealing with morning sickness. The crackers and cheese helped her feel a bit better, but she was anxious to get home. Fatigue was beginning to set in. Moments later she summoned Nina from the playground and headed home.

Marc unloaded the car and took everything into the nursery. With only minor encouragement he persuaded Valerie to go take a nap before dinner. Grandma was still unable to speak due to the pain in her throat, but her eyes were beginning to sparkle like they normally did. When the time came, Nina helped her dad fix dinner while she explained in great detail her shopping day with mom. By the time dinner was ready Valerie was still fast asleep, so Marc let her be. He wrapped a plate for her and not long after cleaning up dinner Valerie came down to eat.

The day had been so busy Nina hadn't even thought about the music box or Sovanna. The following day would be much of the same. First they removed the tags from all the purchases, then Nina helped fold all the freshly washed items and finally she spent some time reading storybooks to Grandma who was showing more improvement. Nina had almost forgotten she had to go back to school. It wasn't until Marc said it was bath time because tomorrow was school did she remember.

Bedtime came earlier on school nights, but Nina didn't mind. It had been quite the couple of weeks. As she drifted off to sleep she recalled happy memories from her Christmas break. Her dreams were filled with happy thoughts, to the point of making her verbally giggle in her sleep. Nina's deep slumber kept her from noticing another one of her fears making its way across her bedroom floor. It was quite possible that even if she were awake she wouldn't have caught sight of the tiny creature crawling under her bed. Little did she know Amos was planning on using this exact fear the next time he challenged her courage. He was arrogantly sure of himself. Amos believed without a shadow of a doubt that his next attempt to conquer Sovanna couldn't fail.

<u>Battle On</u>

It took a few days to get back into the rhythm of school, but soon enough Nina readjusted to her school time routine. Early to bed, early to rise, snack after school, then homework before playtime, followed by dinner and repeat the following day. Weekends had become a time to relax and enjoy family outings, as long as the weather agreed.

To Nina's dismay she awoke on Saturday morning to pouring rain. She could see a river of water rushing down her street and puddles all over the yard. So much for going to the park today. Shuffling down the hall to the stairs revealed Nina's disappointment with the weather. Her shuffling continued into the kitchen where Valerie was busy preparing a big breakfast. Marc was sitting at the table and requested Nina stop dragging her feet.

"I know you're disappointed that we can't go to the park, but I'm sure we can find something fun to do today," Valerie said positively.

Marc added, "Perhaps Grandma will come over too."

Nina gave a weak smile. It had been an exceptionally long wet season. The rain started earlier than normal and there was so much more than usual. It had ruined several family plans and Nina had more than enough of it. How she longed to feel the warmth of the sun on her face, to see bright blue skies and just be able to go outside without an umbrella.

Valerie had outdone herself. There were homemade waffles with diced strawberries, blueberries and whipped cream to enjoy. Scrambled eggs covered in melted cheese, crispy hash browns, bacon and sausage patties. On the table sat the syrup and extra toppings. Her parents added green chilies, mushrooms and spinach to their eggs, but the only thing Nina added to her plate was more fruit for her waffles. The breakfast helped her feel better and when Grandma arrived it helped raise her spirits even more.

While watching a favorite family movie Nina let her mind wander. She thought about school, her friends and eventually she ended up thinking about her friends in Sovanna. She missed them so much and wondered if they were all okay? Was it raining there too? Had Amos attacked the ranch?

"No, Amos can't attack the ranch unless he triumphs over you," answered Roo.

A startled Nina looked around and realized she was back at the ranch. Sunset was filling the sky with various shades of red, orange and yellow. It was beautiful and for a brief moment Nina closed her eyes letting the setting sun warm her face. The weather was so much better in Sovanna then it was at home. Even as the light from the sun faded the air felt warm and comforting. "That was weird," was all Nina said when she opened her eyes.

"Weird?" questioned Roo with a lighthearted tone.

"I was sitting on the floor watching a movie with my family. They're sure to notice I'm gone," explained a concerned Nina.

Roo smiled and simply said, "They won't notice. I just wanted to remind you we're all safe until the final battle between you and Amos."

"When is....." before Nina could finish her question she was back on the floor in her house and the movie was in the exact same place it was when she left. She turned to look at her family and they just smiled back at her.

After that she couldn't focus on the movie. Thoughts of a final battle kept her distracted. She felt that way the rest of the day. The only positive take away from Roo's comment was the word "final." She took it as there was only one more battle against Amos, but was she right in thinking that? No matter how much coloring, game playing or movie watching they did, Amos haunted every waking moment of her day. By the time evening came Nina was frustrated, anxious and exhausted. In an effort to brighten her daughter's mood Valerie reminded Nina that Valentine's Day was only a couple weeks away. She suggested they go look for Valentine cards to give away at school before all the good ones were gone. Nina agreed and when bedtime came she fell asleep with that happy thought running through her mind.

Hours passed peacefully with the entire house sound asleep. It wasn't until Nina felt a tickle on her arm did she move. Still half asleep she scratched her arm. Minutes later another tickle made her scratch the same spot. This time the itching didn't go away and it seemed to be moving from one spot to another. As she scratched harder Nina became more alert. Now there were tickling sensations all over her arm, then one on her cheek. Frustrated she scratched her arm and face until she couldn't take it anymore. She sat up in bed but it was too dark to see. She leaned over and brightened the lamp on her nightstand. When she looked at her arm there wasn't anything there. It wasn't red, there wasn't a mosquito bite or rash, so why was she feeling the need to scratch?

Nina was confused as to what was going on but she was far too tired to figure it out during the middle of the night, so she decided to go back to sleep. Leaning over to dim the lamp she knocked her New Year's Eve tiara and necklaces off the nightstand. At first she thought she'd pick them up in the morning, but a nagging feeling told her to do it now. Nina couldn't reach them so she climbed out of bed and scooped them up. That's when she noticed a baby spider crawling out from under her bed. No matter how small it was it was still a spider and it frightened her. Strangely though the miniature spider turned away from Nina and ran back under the bed. Nina lifted the bed skirt and peered under her bed. The little spider had disappeared. Feeling confident that such a tiny spider couldn't make its way onto her mattress Nina climbed back into bed. The last thing she saw before dozing off was her tiara and necklaces on her nightstand.

Nina hadn't been asleep for long before she felt her bed shake. It didn't feel like an earthquake; she had experienced an earthquake once on a family vacation. Nina listened for anything out of the ordinary but all was quiet in the house, so she closed her eyes in hopes of going back to sleep. Perhaps she was dreaming and her bed didn't actually shake. The next thing she knew Nina felt her bed trembling beneath her. "Daddy!" hollered Nina now scared by all that was happening.

Marc didn't answer or come into her room. "Daddy! Mommy!" she shrieked over and over. Then there was that voice. Nina knew all too well whose voice was whispering her name. It was Amos. Suddenly her dark room was illuminated and the cause of her bed shaking became visible. More spiders than she had ever seen poured out from under her bed eventually causing her bed skirt to tear in multiple places. As they rushed from beneath her quivering bed frame they rattled it so hard Nina held tight to one of the canopy posts. Clinging to the now violently moving post Nina feared she would fall into the growing ocean of spiders below her.

Nina's bed began to creak and moan as the endless tidal wave of spiders poured from under her bed. The arched canopy broke loose and collapsed to the floor and was promptly buried under the mounting number of spiders. Before long the only thing left of Nina's bed was the bottom half of the bed frame, mattress and the single bed post she clung to. That's when she noticed the tiara and necklaces bouncing on the mattress. She had no idea how they got on the mattress but she was happy to see them. With one hand gripping the bed post she squatted down and reached for her treasures. To an observer her reason for doing so couldn't be explained, but Nina had an idea.

Recently in science class they had studied arachnids, a subject she didn't appreciate much, but one important fact stood out. The items Nina was trying so hard to reach were too far away. No matter how determined Nina was to grab ahold of them she couldn't. Suddenly the bed shuddered hard beneath her. To her delight the unexpected heave from the onslaught of spiders moved the tiara and necklaces closer to her, but still not close enough to touch. That's when Nina noticed the barrage of spiders were filling her room to the point of almost reaching the top of her mattress. Nina was sure the bed and she would be buried under the growing pile of creepy critters in a matter of minutes.

Whether it was the unrivaled fear of being covered in spiders or a heightened level of courage Nina didn't know, but she knew she had one choice. Releasing her death grip on the bed post she fell face down towards the tiara and necklaces. No sooner were they in her hands did Nina sit up on her bed, put the necklaces around her neck and the tiara on her head. She took hold of the necklaces and pulled as many of the oval beads into her hands that she could fit. With an authoritative sound in her voice Nina stated, "Blackbirds, blackbirds come to my rescue!"

All the rhinestones on her necklaces and tiara began to crack and split. They looked like colorful miniature eggs breaking open from the inside out. As the shells of the rhinestones fell away there were tiny little black dots shooting into the air. Then in an instant the dots became blackbirds while the ceiling of her room opened up to a cloud filled sky. From every direction for as far as she could see flocks of various blackbirds raced towards her. The walls of her bedroom dissolved under spiders as they tried to flee. Her bed no longer shook as the influx of the detestable attackers ceased. Before long the bright blue sky was hidden behind the invasion of such a multitude of blackbirds. Those that arrived first began devouring the eight-legged arachnids closest to Nina. As the rest of them reached their destination they too feasted on the spiders. The immeasurable amount of birds went into an eating frenzy until at long last every remaining spider was consumed.

By this time Nina had collapsed back onto her mattress, leaving the blackbirds to finish their work. Between the frightful event and it being the middle of the night in her world she was exhausted. One of the blackbirds landed next to her and said, "The coast is clear Miss Nina. Every single spider has been removed." Nina believed he had chosen his words carefully, as she had been rather grossed out by watching the birds eat the wiggling spiders. She definitely wanted them gone and if eating them was the only way to get rid of them so be it. However, watching the spiders squirm and twitch in the beaks of the birds in a desperate attempt to get away wasn't a pleasant sight. Observing the birds gulping down the disgusting creatures was completely nauseating and by far the most revolting thing Nina had ever seen.

"Thank you so very much....What is your name?" inquired Nina trying to keep her queasy stomach at bay.

"Barnaby, Miss Nina."

"Thank you Barnaby for all your help and please thank all your friends that came to my rescue," expressed a grateful but weary Nina.

"It was our pleasure and if you ever need our assistance again please just call out my name," and with that Barnaby and the other blackbirds flew off in every direction with such power it blew Nina's hair away from her face.

As the final flock disappeared in the distance Nina sat in silence. Her bed was still broken and all that remained of her room was the floor directly under her bed. That's when the faintest sound reached her ears. It was a combination of whimpering and shallow breathing. Barnaby's name was ready on Nina's lips as she slid to the foot of her bed. There on the ground beneath her laid Amos. His fur was patchy making him look like he'd gotten a terribly bad haircut. His eyes were half shut and he labored to breathe. He never made eye contact with Nina, he just laid there fighting for his next breath.

Nina almost felt sorry for him. She didn't know what to do. Did she need to say or do something to make him go away? The music box hadn't sent her home and being a smart girl Nina knew better than to try and help him. He was the enemy after all. If she helped him get well neither she or Sovanna would be safe. Nina understood there was only one way this could end, Amos had to be destroyed. If she didn't destroy him, he would ultimately find a way to destroy her. She had found a way to make the spiders go away but apparently, that wasn't enough. That's when the ground began to rumble again. Nina intently watched as the sandy ground beneath Amos shook violently, but somehow it didn't cause her bed to move. That's when she noticed a bump in the sand. The bump soon turned into a sizeable mound which kept getting bigger and bigger. Soon the sand fell from its peak revealing the massive head of a snake. His head was wide and flat with golden-brown eyes that had a black vertical slit in the center, but the most noticeable feature of the snake was the pointed horns above his eyes.

The wicked looking snake slithered around Amos eyeing Nina with an evil glare. Then in one remarkably quick and fluid motion the snake pulled Amos into the sand sending a fiery plume of smoke and embers into the sky. Nina jumped backwards to stay away from the red-hot cinders floating towards the ground. Instead of landing back on her bed she felt someone's arms catch her. Before she could react, she heard a friendly voice, "You did it Nina! I knew you would!" shouted Roo.

Nina turned her head and sure enough it was Roo keeping her from falling to the ground.

They hugged for a bit before cheers erupted around them, "Hip, hip hooray!!! Hip, hip hooray!!!" the crowd of animals roared. Nina took a bow, then another and yet another. It wasn't until the large crowd parted to let Tarak through did their congratulations cease.

Kumah leaped from Tarak's antlers and jumped towards Nina who picked her up and nuzzled her little friend. Tarak waited patiently as Nina and Kumah reveled in her success. As the other animals began to depart Nina turned her focus to Tarak. "Did I do good?" All the accolades from Roo, Kumah and the others were greatly appreciated, but Tarak's approval meant the most to Nina, even if it wasn't until now that she realized it.

Tarak stepped closer and with a charming smile gave Nina his answer, "You did very well my dear one. I am extremely proud of you and indebted to you for rescuing us all from Amos."

Nina ran to Tarak and hugged his neck with all her might. As she held tight to him a thought entered her mind. When she pulled back Tarak could tell something was weighing on her. The wondering look in his eyes prompted her to speak. "I didn't really conquer my fears. I'm still afraid of drowning, the dark and spiders." Her face had gone from exhilaration to despondent in a matter of moments.

Tarak spoke gently but firmly, "Once you learn to swim you will no longer be afraid of drowning…"

Nina interrupted, "But what…." then quickly stopped when Tarak cleared his throat. "I'm sorry Tarak, please forgive me."

"You are forgiven. Conquering a fear doesn't mean you will never be afraid again. Simply put, it means you found courage in the face of fear. You forced yourself to push through the horror you felt. Nina my dear one, you managed to stand strong and courageously fight against your deepest fears. In your boldness, you used your creative intelligence to send your fears fleeing. That is what courage is my dear one. You are a very brave girl."

"I'm brave?" asked a teary-eyed Nina.

"You are extremely brave and because you were so brave you saved Sovanna from turning into a dark evil place." The look of pure admiration in Tarak's eyes conveyed his gratitude.

Nina hugged Tarak again. She felt the warmth of his body leave and when she opened her eyes she was in her bed hugging one of her pillows. Her room was dark except for the dimmed light on her nightstand. She brightened the light and checked to see if her room had been repaired. It had. Then just in case she checked the floor for spiders before seeing if her parents were awake. They were still sound asleep so Nina climbed back into bed not believing there was any chance of falling back to sleep, but it only took a moment before Nina dozed off.

Twists and Turns

Over the next couple of weeks Nina spent as much time as possible in Sovanna. She and Roo were becoming the very best of friends. Between their combined imaginations they never seemed to run out of adventures to go on. They had traveled to outer space where they explored the galaxy on shooting stars, spent a great deal of time visiting mermaid villages, were acrobats in a circus performing impossible feats with a lion as ring master and even traveled to see the dinosaurs, who of course were extremely friendly and talkative. Each of them had even ridden a dinosaur of their choosing in a race. The real world had become a bit mundane in comparison, but Nina was always excited to return to her loving family.

Back in her world Nina got busy completing her Valentine's Day cards for her classmates, but Tiffany's card was the only one with a special note written on the back. That gave Nina a wonderful idea, she filled out another card with a much longer note written on the back and stuffed it in an envelope. Inside the large heart that she drew Nina wrote the name Roo.

"Are you about finished?" asked Valerie.

Nina slid Roo's card under the rest and said, "I just finished."

"Good job. I'll get a bag for you to put them in and then you can put them in your backpack so you don't forget them on Monday."

While Valerie went to get a bag, Nina tucked Roo's card into the waistband of her pants and pulled her shirt over top of it. After all the other cards were packed in the brown lunch bag Nina took them upstairs. She confirmed her dad was still outside trying to cut the damp grass and Valerie was busy on the phone with Grandma, then Nina headed into her parent's room.

"Hello," she said to the quiet piano music box. To her disappointment nothing happened. The music box was still out of reach so Nina was dependent on her parents winding it up or for the music box to wind itself, and there was no rhyme or reason as to when that happened. "Please play your music," begged Nina. Still nothing. "Play me a tale," pleaded Nina. If only she could reach it. Nina looked around the room for something to stand on. Every part of her knew she would be in trouble if she got caught trying to wind the piano herself, but she felt desperate.

"May I ask what you are doing missy?" asked a sweet unfamiliar voice.

Nina spun around and sitting on the headboard of her parent's bed was a pure white dove. The bird rephrased her question, "Nina, what are you trying to do?"

Nina rambled without completing a single sentence. She had been caught and there was nothing she could say to change that. Nina ended her incoherent rambling and admitted, "I was trying to reach the piano."

"Are you supposed to touch the piano?"

"No," whispered Nina with her head down low, feeling ashamed.

The dove flew closer to Nina and said, "Thank you for being honest. Now would you tell me why you were going to break the rules and do something you know you shouldn't?"

"Because..." Nina knew her excuses weren't going to help. She thought for a moment and admitted, "I thought I wouldn't get caught."

"There it is, the full truth," said the dove. "Perhaps a lesson in integrity is in order. Do you know what integrity means?"

"Being good?" Nina replied hoping she was right.

"In part. Integrity means being honest and having high morals. Let me put this in a way you can better understand. Morality means you know the difference between right and wrong, good and bad. Having integrity helps someone do what's right no matter the situation. Whether that person is by themselves or with a crowd of people they do the right thing."

"Do you understand?" inquired Tarak.

Nina lifted her face finding herself at the ranch. "I understand. I was wrong and I won't let it happen again."

The dove was perched on Tarak's antlers and chimed in, "We expect nothing less," and with that she took to the air.

Tarak added to her words, "We cannot accept anything less my dear one. You must always behave with integrity."

Picking up on the subtle inflection in Tarak's voice Nina knew it was a warning and asked, "Is Amos coming back?"

"No you took care of him."

"But?" pressed Nina.

"You will find out soon enough. Until then remember and hold tight to your integrity lesson."

Before Nina could say another word, she was returned to her parent's room. She pushed her mom's vanity stool back where it belonged and went to her room. Nina tucked Roo's Valentine's card in her sock drawer for safe keeping. That's when she heard a car door slam and her dad welcoming someone to the house. Peering out her window she saw Tiffany and her mom talking to Marc. Seeing Tiffany lifted her spirits after being caught doing something she knew was wrong. Nina ran downstairs and out the front door in her bare feet, "Hi Tiffany!" she shouted from the porch.

Tiffany ran towards her and handed her a little stuffed heart with the letters "BFF" embroidered on it. "I didn't want to give you this on Monday in front of the class so I brought it today." Nina was overjoyed with her gift, but that was soon overpowered by her guilt for not having something special for Tiffany. That's when Valerie joined them outside. Her hands were behind her back and she whispered in Nina's ear, "Here you go." Nina took what her mom was handing her with her back towards Tiffany. With a quick glance Nina saw it was a small pink frog with red hearts covering its body. Nina kissed her mom's cheek, said thank you and turned back to Tiffany. "My mom thought this stuffed frog was perfect for you. Because you have a waterfall and pond in your backyard." Nina correctly gave her mom all the credit, after all she was the one who saved the day.

"It's perfect!" squealed Tiffany who hugged the frog tightly while adding, "We should have tadpoles soon." The girls didn't get to talk much as Tiffany's mom called her to leave because they had other errands to take care of. The girls said their goodbye's then Nina and Valerie headed inside.

"Thank you Mom. I forgot about getting Tiffany a Valentine gift this year." Her tone expressed her shame. Exchanging Valentine gifts with Tiffany had begun when they were in the same kindergarten class. This was the first-time Nina had forgotten their Valentine habit.

"You're very welcome. I picked it up one day when you were at school. I guess it slipped your mind this year, but I'm sure it won't happen again."

"No, it won't. It was my idea when I was five so it's really bad that I forgot."

Valerie took her daughter into her arms and explained that everyone makes mistakes, but the important thing to remember is to learn from them. Her mom's advice helped Nina feel better about almost hurting Tiffany's feelings. Perhaps that was why she had an integrity lesson earlier. Was it possible Nina would have lied and taken the credit for Tiffany's gift? Either way Nina was going to be more careful about remembering things. When Nina got back to her room she closed her eyes and silently took an oath to never forget her integrity lesson.

The following afternoon Valerie and Nina headed to Grandma's place. Arriving with lunch they walked in to see boxes on the living room floor and scattered pictures on the coffee and dining table.

"Let's eat lunch on the patio. I don't want to mess up all my separating," suggested Theresa.

Nina finished her quesadilla before her mom and grandma finished their taco plates. "Can I go look at the pictures?" Nina asked.

Theresa agreed, "Of course, but please don't move any of them around. It may not look like it but they're in groups that go together."

Valerie told Nina they were there to help Grandma put her photo's in albums to keep them safe and organized. After telling them she wouldn't mess them up Nina went inside. She first looked over the pictures on the coffee table. It was strange to see pictures void of any colors. There wasn't anyone she recognized in the photos making her less than interested in them. Before moving on to the dining table Nina hollered, "Why isn't there any color in the pictures. Didn't people have any other color clothes but gray, black and white?"

This made Theresa and Valerie laugh so hard they could barely speak. Theresa caught her breath first and explained that there was color back then, but the cameras could only take pictures in black and white. Nina didn't fully understand what that meant and with a shrug she walked over to the dining table.

She climbed up on one of the chairs and began searching for a face she recognized. Nope, not one familiar face in the bunch. Nina moved to another chair and the moment she looked down at the picture in front of her she was astonished. "Roo?" she mumbled. Nina lifted the photo to her face confirming it was Roo. She wasn't at the ranch, but Nina was positive it was Roo. Nina wondered why Roo would be in Grandma's old pictures, but before she could dwell on that question she wanted to see if Roo were in any other photos.

Nina put the photo back where it was and standing on the chair studied a bigger radius of the pictures. Time and time again she found Roo in them. Riding a horse, fishing in a stream, learning to roll out tortillas and one of her taking a bath in a large tub with feet on it. Nina had never seen such a strange looking tub. One particular picture stood out above the rest. It was Roo standing next to a woman who was handing her the piano music box.

Nina didn't recognize the woman, but she was beautiful with waist length wavy hair and a smile that drew you in. Who was giving Roo the music box? It was probably her mother, but Nina wondered if it were someone else, perhaps someone from Sovanna. Just then Valerie and

Theresa came inside and in unison asked, "What did you find?"

Nina was speechless. She couldn't ask who was giving Roo the music box. There was no possible way to explain how she recognized Roo. Grandma walked over to Nina and looked at the photo in her hand. With a smile Theresa said, "That's my mom when she was a little girl......and her mother." In the span of that sentence Theresa's voice went from happy recollection to sadness. Her next words clarified why, "My grandmother died when I was only three months old. Somewhere there's a single picture of her holding me before her death."

Valerie looked at her mom with compassion and rubbed her shoulder while asking to see the photo of Grandma Ruth as a little girl. Valerie thought to herself how terribly sad it was that her mom never knew her grandma. To this day Valerie cherished the memories of her Grandma Ruth. In an effort to lighten the mood Valerie stated, "My goodness Nina, you sure look a lot like your Great-Grandma Ruth did when she was little."

"I agree," chimed in Theresa sounding better. "Look on the back, it has my mom's nickname Roo written on it." That was the last straw. Nina felt faint and wobbled on the chair she was standing on. "Careful jellybean," was all Grandma said.

Nina didn't answer. Her mind was buzzing with a multitude of questions and her belly felt nauseous. All this time she had been playing with her Great-Grandma Ruth when she was a little girl? Nothing made sense and the more Nina tried to make it make sense the worst she felt. Excusing herself to the bathroom Nina washed her face in cold water to try and help the shock wear off. Sitting on the side of the tub Nina went through her visits with Roo bringing up one clear question. Was it possible Roo knew she'd been playing with her great-granddaughter all this time?

"Are you alright in there?" Nina's mom asked knocking on the door. Nina assured her she was and would be right out.

She came out just in time to hear her mom ask Theresa a question. "How did Grandma end up with the nickname Roo?"

Theresa smiled fondly then explained, "The youngest son of the family that lived next door to my grandparents couldn't say her name. No matter how hard the little boy tried it always came out as Roo and it just stuck."

Theresa and Valerie continued their conversation and soon Nina joined them asking, "Are there any more pictures of Great-Grandma when she was little?"

"There sure are," cheered Theresa thrilled Nina seemed so interested in her great-grandma.

It was clear Grandma had been working hard on organizing her photos. The pictures of Roo gradually went from her as a young girl, to a teenager, followed by stunning wedding photos. Although the pictures were black and white Nina could envision how beautiful the flower garden they stood in must have been. The next photo Theresa held up was of Great-Grandma Ruth holding an infant in front of a small house.

Grandma explained it was her as an infant, which Nina had already figured out. At last they got to one of Nina's absolute favorites. A picture of Great-Grandma Ruth handing the piano to Theresa when she was a young girl.

Nina was thankful her mom asked the nagging question running through her mind. "Do you know if Grandma Ruth's mother received the music box from her mom?"

"I'm not sure. As far as I know no one knows who originally owned the music box. To the best of my knowledge the picture of my mom receiving it from her mother is the first photo showing the exchange." Theresa turned to Nina, "That picture proves it's been in our family for at least five generations. It's a shame no one remembers who the original owner was, but either way it's a very special keepsake and when you turn ten we will take a picture of you receiving it."

Nina smiled and simply replied, "On my tenth birthday, right?" Theresa confirmed that was correct and then the work of putting the pictures inside photo albums began.

By the time Nina and her mom arrived home Nina was mentally drained. Part of her wanted to go visit with Roo, but a much larger part of her understood she didn't have the strength to do so. Nina had no idea how to handle this new information and what ramifications it could have. It did explain why Nina felt so very close to Roo and how easy it was for Roo to all but replace Tiffany as her best friend. That epiphany clued Nina in on why and how she had forgotten to buy a gift for Tiffany. In Nina's heart Roo had clearly become the very best friend she had ever had. However, she hadn't been able to admit that to herself and she sure couldn't reveal that to anyone else. There wasn't a single person in the real world that Nina could tell Roo was now her "BFF" over Tiffany. She had to keep the magical world hidden at all costs and that included her knowledge of Roo.

Those thoughts led to even more unanswered questions. Was it their family bond that made them such good friends? Perhaps it was the magic of the music box or all the unimaginable escapades they shared. Thoughts darted through

Nina's brain as she struggled to piece together everything she had learned. Sleep evaded her for hours until fatigue overpowered her wandering mind.

The Bottom Line

Nina tossed and turned throughout the night. In her restless sleep, she recalled the black and white photos of her great-grandma. She remembered how lovely Gram looked on her wedding day and how handsome her great-grandpa was. Nina had only seen a few photos of him in their family albums and he looked nothing like the young good-looking groom when he wed Gram. He had battled cancer for years and as his body succumbed to the illness he grew frail and emaciated. Nina, like most children never considered her great-grandpa was once young, healthy and full of life.

Nina rolled over in bed feeling far too tired to get up for school, but her mom pressed on. "It's time to get up and get ready," urged Valerie, but Nina just laid there motionless. "I guess you'll just have to miss out on all the fun at school. It's a shame you're going to miss your class Valentine's Day party," baited Valerie turning to leave. As expected the ploy worked. Nina sat up, rubbed her eyes and slid out of bed.

Nina put on her black long sleeve shirt with a large white outline of a heart on the front. Inside the contour of the large heart were tiny glitter covered ruby red hearts. She chose her bright red boots to complete her outfit. "Happy Valentine's Day!" cheered Nina as she greeted her mom downstairs. Valerie had added red and white streamers to the small cork board in the kitchen that usually held notes, a shopping list and other reminders, but today front and center was Nina's artwork from school. It was a cut out of a bear holding a heart that read, "Happy Valentine's Day. I love you Mom and Dad."

"Happy Valentine's Day," replied Valerie giving Nina a big hug and a kiss on the cheek. There was a bright pink bag on the counter with white tissue paper sticking out of it and Nina knew it was for her, but she'd have to wait until her dad got home from work to open it. When Nina was dropped off at school it was clearly a festive day. Most of the kids were in red or pink, they all had bags full of cards to hand out and parents carried goodies for the parties. Nina no longer felt tired. She was beyond excited for the fun-filled day ahead of her, then something popped into her head. She could hardly wait to give Roo her Valentine's Day card and wondered what Sovanna did to celebrate this special day. She forced that thought aside as she spotted Tiffany running towards her.

After the class parties the students were amped up on all the sugary treats, so outside they went. The sugar rush had them running, jumping, chasing and doing anything but sitting still. The teachers kept watch for trouble, but for the most part the kids were just burning off their overabundant energy supply. By the time school let out the majority of them had rosy red cheeks from all their activities. Keeping the children outside to burn off their exuberance not only served the teachers but the parents as well. As Nina and her mom walked home she began dragging her feet, which Valerie kindly yet firmly put an end to. The sugar crash was well on its way and soon after arriving home Nina was sound asleep on the couch, having gone through only about half of her Valentine cards.

Waking to the smell of dinner Nina stretched and yawned before sitting up. Almost as if on cue Marc came through the door. He held a bouquet of fragrant flowers in one hand and in the other a box of dark chocolate candy with various nuts. Marc greeted Valerie with a lengthy hug and a sweet kiss before leaning over and speaking to Valerie's growing belly, "Happy Valentine's Day little one." Then Marc's attention fell on Nina. With wide open arms, he greeted his daughter, lifted her up in a bear hug and said, "Happy Valentine's Day."

Upon finishing their yummy meal Nina knew it was time for her to open her present. Simultaneously the doorbell rang when Marc picked up her gift. Holding the gift in his hand he went to see who was at the door. Nina knew that voice, it was Grandma. What a wonderful surprise. Nina ran to greet her and was handed a small wrapped box after receiving her traditional hello hug. Marc suggested Nina open Grandma's gift first so she obliged. Nina opened the little white box and gasped at the sight. It was a silver necklace with a beautiful open heart charm hanging from one of its sides with a tiny pink gem on the opposite end. Nina's excitement was evident in her eyes and she quickly asked her mom to put it on her.

Nina rushed to the bathroom to look at the wonderful gift. Beaming with delight Nina viewed her reflection from several angles feeling so proud to have what she considered a grown-up necklace. "Look how pretty it is!" cheered Nina when she returned. That's when she noticed the bag Marc had been holding sitting front and center on the dining table. Without saying a word her eyes communicated her question.

"Go ahead. Open your gift," Valerie prompted, before adding, "Please be very careful."

Nina opted against tossing the tissue paper to the floor. Instead she gently lifted each piece from the bag, sitting it on the table. Standing on her chair she peered inside the bag. Whatever was inside was wrapped in more layers of tissue. Her parents were alert to every move Nina made as she lifted the rather weighty gift, for its size, from the bag. Much to her relief the tissue was gathered on the top with only a few pieces of tape holding it closed. Once again Nina was reminded to be careful.

With painstaking movements Nina removed the tape and delicately opened the tissue paper. She couldn't believe her eyes. Astonishment covered her face as she stared at the magical music box. Pure elation filled every cell in her being. She looked up at her family with wide eyes and said, "You're giving me Gram's piano?" but before they could answer she pointed out the obvious, "I'm not ten."

"We know," concurred Valerie, "But we discussed it and we believe you have proven yourself worthy to receive it a bit early. It's a big responsibility and we expect you to make us proud."

Nina promised, "Oh I will Mom. I'll take extra special care of it."

Grandma chimed in, "Something made us feel like it already belonged to you, jellybean."

Valerie nodded in agreement before reminding Nina of all the rules for taking care of her new treasure. Nina once again assured her mom that she would take very good care of the music box. Although neither her mom or grandma believed in the magic the piano still held, Nina knew all too well of its very real existence. Damaging the music box meant she would never again see Roo. That was something she wanted to avoid at all costs. Nina vowed to herself to be extra careful with the piano. The mere thought of never seeing Roo again made her heart hurt. Besides being fearful over losing Roo, Nina was concerned that the multitude of unsettling questions in her head would forever remain unanswered.

When bedtime rolled around Nina made the wise choice to have Marc carry the music box upstairs. He placed her cherished gift on top of her dresser towards the back and close to the wall. It was safe from being accidentally bumped, but close enough that Nina could reach it and wind it up if she stood on her desk chair. Nina laid in bed reliving the best Valentine's Day she'd ever had. Thrilled about wearing her heart necklace to school Nina plucked it from her nightstand. Even in the dim light the necklace shimmered in beauty. Rolling over after putting the necklace down Nina's eyes locked on the music box. It sat there silently in stark contrast to her mind, which was frantically racing through countless scenarios of her future in Sovanna. She didn't know what impact discovering Roo's true identity would have, but Nina was sure of one thing. It had to have changed everything.

Far off in the distance Nina could hear the faint tune of the music box. Shifting from one position to another Nina felt uneasy as she struggled to remain asleep. An internal struggle was going on as part of Nina wanted to wake up and the other part just wanted to sleep. This had never happened before. She usually couldn't wait to return to the magical world and yet this black cloud hung over her as she feared how different things might be in Sovanna. Suddenly a bitterly cold gust of wind blew through her room making her shoot up in bed. With wide eyes, she searched her bedroom for anyone or anything, but it was just her alone in her room.

The muffled far off sound of the music box clearly wasn't coming from the actual music box. Nina even climbed out of bed to verify the piano was silent and sure enough it wasn't making a sound. Turning to get back in bed altered her bedroom. Systematically her room was transformed into what appeared to be the interior of a castle. Nina wasn't sure she was standing in a castle, but based on the various princess movies she had seen it seemed plausible.

Tarak came through the massive doorway saying, "My dear one would you follow me?"

There was a heightened level of grandeur about him. With a slight nod Nina walked towards him. It wasn't until she took her first step that she noticed she was wearing some sort of gown. The alabaster dress was floor length with a laced bodice and sleeves. Embroidered on the bodice were a multitude of golden beads. They shimmered in the sun's rays coming through the large balcony doors. Their shine reminded Nina of the music box when the sunlight hit it.

Feeling very much like a princess Nina found herself standing taller, walking more deliberately and gracefully moving her hand when she took hold of the handrail at the top of the expansive stairway. When she finally reached the bottom Tarak continued to walk in silence towards a set of oversized double doors. The rich mahogany wood was dressed in an intricate design of iron swirls peeling from what looked like metal arrows. The arch of the doorway came to a peak at the center. As Tarak approached the doors, they magically opened. Tarak strutted through them with lots of room to spare. The gigantic doorway left ample space for Tarak and his large rack of antlers.

At the far end of the immense room sat a king on a wooden throne inlayed with gold vines on the front legs and along the edges of the towering back. As Nina drew closer to the king he remained silent and increased in size. He and his throne were becoming quite enormous. The walls of the large room were solid gold reflecting not only Tarak and herself but the king on his throne. That's when she noticed the arm rest, front and back legs of the throne were one ornately carved panel. Nina was sure it was to hold the weight of the ever-growing king. Centered on the intricate peak of the throne, high above the king's crown was a golden dragon head.

Tarak bowed low before the king prompting Nina to follow suit. Standing before the colossal king made Nina imagine that was how Kumah felt next to her. With coal black eyes the king stared at Nina in silence. Feeling uneasy by the continued silence Nina began to shiver with apprehension. That's when the king winked at her in a playful manner before flashing her an endearing smile. He reached out his massive hand and gently asked Nina to climb into it. Tarak's reassuring glance gave Nina the courage to do so. Once again she was brave in the face of fear.

Standing in the king's hand gave Nina the chance to examine him closer. His dark eyes had a softness to them and although his shoulder length hair, mustache and beard were snowy white he had a youthful appearance. His dignified multi-peaked crown was covered in colorful gems reminding Nina of her New Year's Eve tiara, even if it were a weak comparison. The king wore an emerald green tunic with a matching gold dragon head embroidered in the center of the cross-like pattern on his chest. His imperial mantle was gray in color trimmed in white fur. His capelet was completely covered in white fur pulling together his royal attire. He waited patiently as Nina inspected him.

No sooner did her eyes meet his did he speak, "My name is King Alroi." Nina wasn't sure if he were whispering, but thankfully his voice didn't rattle her bones as expected.

"I'm Nina," she declared.

"Yes. I know who you are."

Before she could stop the words from escaping her lips she asked, "Am I in trouble?" It was too late. She was sure the king was going to answer her, but she wasn't sure she wanted to know the answer to her blurted question.

"No," was all he said before looking over at Tarak. "Perhaps it would be best if your guardian explained."

"Guardian," thought Nina being reminded that was Tarak's role. Tarak had become so much more than her guardian, he was a trusted friend and confidant, not to mention her magical instructor.

Tarak didn't pull any punches and point blank told Nina what was wrong. "Now that you know Roo is your great-grandma we are faced with a difficult situation."

"I didn't mean to find out!" Nina shrilled.

King Alroi interjected, "We are aware you were not the cause; however, the issue must be addressed."

"How?" questioned Nina. Was she to be banned from returning to Sovanna? The mere thought of that almost brought her to tears, especially since she had just been given the music box. Her emotions got the best of her, "I know I got the music box before my tenth birthday. Can I just give it back? Would that fix it?"

Tarak responded with tenderness in his voice, "No my dear one. The situation is far more complicated than that."

"What do I need to do?" Nina inquired, feeling she alone had the power to fix the problem she never intended to create. "Why didn't you stop me from finding out Roo is Gram?" cried a broken-hearted Nina.

"We have limited control of your world Nina," King Alroi proclaimed before continuing. "Freewill can move in unexpected ways causing unforeseen complications. Even if magic were able to detect every potential problem it wouldn't be of much help."

Nina looked puzzled by the king's words, so Tarak explained further. "There was no way for us to stop your grandma from going through her old photos or to keep you from seeing Roo. Such an intrusion into your world could reveal the magical worlds and that is forbidden for the masses."

While hopelessness gripped Nina she listened to Tarak clarify her choices. "You and you alone must choose between the very real risk of continuing to visit Sovanna or making the decision to never again see Roo." Tarak had just confirmed she had what felt like an impossible choice to make. Then things got worse. "If you decide to keep visiting Roo, you must never under any circumstance let her know she is your great-grandmother. If Roo were to ever uncover the truth of your relationship to her it would forever alter the world as you know it. A simple slip of the tongue would change the lives of so many."

King Alroi explicitly told Nina, "If Roo discovered the truth about who you are, it could drastically change not only the course of Roo's life but the lives of your parents and your grandparent's. In all likelihood, the knowledge of her future would alter her life to the point of it being unrecognizable."

"What does that mean?" pleaded Nina.

Tarak tried to soothe Nina's nerves by saying, "Nina I know this is a lot to take in, but time-travel is tricky and comes with a great deal of risks. Learning anything about one's future routinely causes significant alterations to that future."

"What?" muttered Nina as tears welled in her eyes. Neither the king's or Tarak's words were helping her understand the problem.

"Nina, not only would you presumably cease to exist, your mom and grandma would too," replied King Alroi.

Tarak put it more simply, "Roo would probably make different decisions based on knowing you are her great-granddaughter. Even if she deliberately tried not to. Humans can only handle so much and having one's future foretold is substantially more than anyone has been able to handle. No matter how much Roo tried, it's highly probable that you wouldn't be born."

Tears now flowed freely from Nina's eyes. She wasn't at all sure why she wouldn't be born but she needed to know more. "What about my mom and grandma?"

"I expect they too would be gone."

"So my family would disappear?"

"Your family would carry on, but in a different way. The family you know may or may not exist. They would be different versions of themselves or completely different individuals would be born in their place. There is no way to know for certain," confessed Tarak.

This was too much to bear. Nina crumbled to the floor sobbing. Over her sobs she heard King Alroi hint at another course of action. "There is one other choice." Nina lifted her tear-stained face towards the king and waited with baited breath.

Choose a Path

King Alroi leaned over and dropped a handkerchief towards Nina. Fearful the canopy size cloth tissue would completely bury her, Nina covered her head with her arms. Nothing happened. Slowly she lifted her head, to find an appropriate size hankie laying on the floor in front of her. She picked it up and wiped her face before blowing her nose.

Resuming his royal posture the king proposed, "If you choose to never again visit Roo in Sovanna," before pausing for much longer than Nina hoped. "It would prevent her from discovering your identity, thus preventing any changes to the course of events leading to where we are now." Before Nina could open her mouth to speak King Alroi stated, "No. We cannot undo your discovery of Roo being your Gram."

So, where was the alternative? Nina wondered. She had already concluded that choosing to play with Roo could literally change her world in a terrible way. However, never being able to use the music box which now sat on her dresser seemed like a nightmare. Not to mention it sometimes wound itself up. How could she stop that?

"We could magically break the piano," responded the king answering her thoughts. He went on to say that's what happened with her grandma and mom. Once they stopped believing in magic the music box ceased to work and it was by his hand. Then he said something she didn't expect, "However, I must admit that would be a terrible shame. We truly believe you will follow in the footsteps of your Great-Grandma Ruth. It is quite possible you will never stop believing in magic."

Losing her patience Nina admitted, "I don't see another choice," then blurted rather harshly, "If there is one, just tell me what it is?" Nina quickly added, "Please, please tell me the other choice," in an effort to smooth over her rather curt request. Nina had never showed this level of disrespect to anyone. No matter how dreadful her circumstances she knew there wasn't any excuse for her behavior.

King Alroi locked eyes with Nina but didn't say a word until she apologized for snapping at him. He said she was forgiven but cautioned her not to let it happen again. Nina promised. Tarak's look was all that was needed for Nina to rise to her feet. Standing in silence she waited for the king. She didn't fidget or look around, she knew better than to test the king's authority a second time. It wasn't fear that kept her stationary, it was respect.

At last King Alroi spoke and offered an alternate choice, "You could make the choice to only use the music box to visit your Gram."

Nina wanted confirmation, "Gram? As an old lady? I mean Roo is my Gram, only as a little girl."

"Yes. It would mean you could only visit your Gram as an adult. At that point in her life it's too late to change her marriage to your great-grandfather or the events that led to your grandma's, mother's and your birth."

"And my baby brother or sister," whispered Nina.

"That is correct," King Alroi confirmed. "Your sibling would still be on their way."

Then Nina remembered Gram saying she couldn't see her any more so this option seemed out of the question. "But Gram said I couldn't visit her anymore."

"As long as you were visiting Roo that is correct," King Alroi affirmed.

"Why?"

King Alroi pulled something from under his imperial mantle, but Nina couldn't tell what is was. He reached out his hand where she could see something hanging from one of his tree trunk size fingers. Tarak stepped forward as the king let what appeared to be a massive necklace drop off his finger. As the twinkling chain quickly descended to the floor it dramatically changed in size. The chain was caught on a single tine of Tarak's antlers. Tarak offered the necklace to Nina. After lifting the piece of jewelry from the tine Nina examined it closely. Hanging at the bottom of the delicate gold chain was a gold oval pendant. The front of the pendant had a stunningly beautiful painting of a young woman seated on something which her long full-dress covered. Nina was amazed at the level of detail in the miniature painting. The woman's right arm was lifted to eye level and upon a closer look Nina spotted a butterfly fluttering around the woman's hand. Soon the butterfly landed on her palm and that's when the woman turned her smiling face at Nina.

"It's like the piano!" bubbled Nina. She wasn't sure what it meant, but she understood the necklace in her hand was another magical item. After examining the pendant closer Nina realized the painting looked very much like the painting on the piano lid. Then a memory shot into her head. Each time she had visited Gram she was wearing this very necklace. All except the last time Nina saw her. Nina hadn't thought much about it at the time, but now she figured it meant something. "This is Gram's necklace."

"Well done," beamed King Alroi.

Tarak smiled proudly, "I knew you would remember it."

"Why do you have her necklace?" inquired Nina hoping the answer would help her put the jumbled mess of questions in her head to rest.

"I must tend to another matter. Tarak will explain," was all the king said. King Alroi vanished into nothingness before their eyes. Nina then found herself on the balcony of the room in which she had first arrived. Nina could hardly believe her eyes. The balcony she and Tarak stood on was near the top of the highest turret of the castle. Doing her best to take in the magnitude and beauty of the royal palace soon took second place when she noticed the castle was ever so slowly rotating between opposing cliffs. Below she could see an enormous lapis blue river making its way between the picturesque landscape. Hanging from below the rocky terrain of the expansive castle were thick lush vines covered in multicolored neon flowers. The flowers danced and shimmered so brightly Nina couldn't look at them for too long.

"Are we floating?" Nina asked.

"Yes we are. Look up," suggested Tarak.

The sky was filled with an overabundance of stars and the moons were all draped in lavender clouds. It wasn't like anything Nina had ever seen. It appeared to be night, but a golden glow from behind the cliffs gave the illusion that it was daytime without stripping the night sky of its majesty. "Where are we?"

"That is of no significance dear one."

"Please tell me," implored Nina.

"We are in the kingdom of King Alroi. That is all you need to know," answered Tarak. "Now let me answer your question about why King Alroi has your Gram's pendant."

Nina had all but forgotten her question. Gripping her Gram's necklace tighter she asked, "Yes, please. Why is my Gram's necklace here?"

"Do you remember me using the words portal and gateway?"

"Yes," answered Nina before adding, "That's how I get from my world to the magical world and back again."

"Very good." Tarak thought for a moment then asked, "Do you use a key to open the front door of your home?" Nina nodded in the affirmative. "Think of the piano music box and your Gram's necklace as keys. Those two keys can open the portals to magical worlds."

"So there's more than one magical world?" wondered Nina. Even her impressive imagination hadn't given thought to that possibility.

"There are more magical worlds than you could count and King Alroi oversees them all. Now back to the portals. Each key unlocks a specific magical world by way of a portal."

"So without a key no one can get in or out?"

"Precisely my dear one. In order for you or anyone else to travel through a gateway into a specific magical world they need a key."

This new unexpected news was exciting, but it still didn't explain why King Alroi had Gram's necklace. "So why is Gram's key here?" repeated Nina.

Tarak took a deep breath before proceeding, "King Alroi wanted it here for safe keeping until you made your decision about Sovanna."

"I don't understand," sighed Nina.

"Your Gram understood how risky it could have been for you to visit her as a girl and as your Gram. It increased the chances of something going wrong," replied Tarak who went on to say if Nina ever invited Roo to visit Gram it would have caused an irreversible time paradox. Nina wasn't sure what that was, but between Tarak's cautionary tone and forewarning gaze she understood it to be very very bad.

Another issue Nina hadn't given any thought to came to mind. She'd been so enthralled with her magical visits that she never really cared how it all worked. "How is it possible for me to visit Gram when she's old and when she's young?"

In a direct tone Tarak answered, "Not only does each magical world have its own gateway keys, each world has their own space-time." The bewilderment on Nina's face was increasing so Tarak tried to help by getting straight to the point,

"Time travel Nina. You've been traveling through time." Tarak then got back to the subject at hand, "We need you to decide whether you will continue to visit Roo and be diligent in keeping your identity a secret for your own safety or whether you will choose to never again visit Sovanna."

Nina interrupted, "Or chose to visit Gram when she's old."

"Yes. Those are your options."

The answer seemed obvious. If visiting Gram meant her true identity wouldn't change the real world that was a simple choice. Nina's mind was made up. Then an unexpected problem arose. "If I choose Gram I may only have a short time with her because she's going to die."

King Alroi had returned which immediately transported Tarak and Nina back in front of him as he took a seat on his throne. "Yes Nina. Your Gram will die. She will still have passed away in your world." The king gave Nina a moment to soak in what he had said then added, "However, your family will be intact as you know it."

"Then what happens? Will I still be able to travel to the magical world?" Could I ever go back to Sovanna?"

In a gentle but authoritative manner King Alroi stated, "Nina we could spend an eternity trying to work through every possible scenario in magical time travel and still not have all the answers. It's a complicated web of possibilities. Which is why only a select few are ever welcomed in Sovanna or any of the other magical worlds. Your imagination has allowed you this privilege, but your continuous inquiries and delay in making a choice puts your magical bestowment at risk." Nina's face expressed that he had lost her. The king cut to the chase, "You would no longer be welcomed into the magical worlds if you fail to make a decision. No matter how imaginative you remained I would abolish your magical gift. Do you understand?"

"Yes King Alroi," professed Nina.

"Very good. You have until the next full moon in your world to give me your answer," and just like that Nina was back in her bedroom. It was still nighttime making Nina rush to her window. There was a half-moon shining in the dark sky. Nina had no idea how long she had until the moon was full, but did it really matter? If she had a lifetime could she make the decision the king was waiting for? That thought was moot. One way or another a decision had to be made and she understood if she didn't decide King Alroi would choose for her.

Nina's heart broke at the thought of being around when Gram died. Saying goodbye to visiting Gram was difficult enough, but at least Nina believed she was still alive. "She must be alive," Nina told herself. Why else would visiting her be an option?

The only thing Nina was absolutely sure of was she couldn't ever play with Roo again. Destroying her family as she knew it was entirely off the table. Remembering Roo's Valentine's card in her sock drawer made her cry. She would never be able to give it to her. With that tragic thought wandering around her head Nina cried herself to sleep.

Valerie came in to wake Nina for school and found her daughter with swollen eyes. "Wake up bumblebee," cooed Valerie. Nina struggled to open her eyes causing her to vigorously rub them. "Oh no Nina, don't irritate them more. I'll get you a cold compress."

Nina did her best to open her eyes while Valerie was gone. Through the narrow slits in her eyes she looked around at her room. She wasn't sure what had happened. "Mama what's wrong with my eyes?" asked a frightened Nina.

"I'm not sure, but if I didn't know better I would say you were crying all night long."

Little did her mom know she had hit the nail on the head, but Nina couldn't tell her that's exactly what had happened, so she said nothing. Thankfully Valerie suggested a visit to the doctor later that afternoon if the swelling didn't go down. That meant Nina would be staying home from school. What a wonderful turn of events. Attending school with such a life-changing decision looming over her head would have been extremely tough.

By the time Nina had brushed her teeth and hair the slits in her eyes had widen a bit. With great care, she made her way down the stairs where Valerie was on the phone with the school informing them Nina would not be there. Valerie offered to make Nina some breakfast but her flip flopping tummy didn't want any food. Nina ended up on the couch with her head resting on her mom's lap.

Nina fell asleep so Valerie took the morning to watch a little television and enjoy some alone time with her sleepy daughter. When the movie was almost over Nina stretched, and yawned before opening her eyes wide open. She looked up at Valerie who was thrilled to see her daughter's eyes were back to normal. After lunch they played a couple games before heading upstairs to the nursery. With a new coat of paint, baby furniture and fairy tale themed artwork the nursery was coming together nicely. Valerie and Nina worked on finding a place for all the clothes, toys and supplies.

Standing back to admire their hard work made them smile in anticipation of the newest family member. Valerie quickly grabbed Nina's hand and placed it on her stomach saying, "The baby is kicking." Nina waited in silence. She desperately wanted to feel her younger sibling kick, but nothing happened. Disappointment filled Nina when Valerie shrugged her shoulders. The sound of Marc arriving home broke the moment and they headed downstairs to greet him.

During dinner Valerie told Marc all about Nina's swollen eyes and the rest of their day. Marc was very happy to see Nina was back to normal and had been such a big help with setting up the nursery. Marc asked Nina if she wanted to join him outside when they finished their meal. He had something special to show her. Naturally she agreed and her excitement grew when he explained he had spotted a bird's nest in a tree when he left for work.

Marc lifted Nina high above his head and told her where to look. Nina spotted the cereal bowl size nest in no time, but to her dismay there weren't any eggs inside the nest. "Maybe mama bird hasn't laid them yet. We will keep an eye on the nest and see if she lays some. I'm sure there'll be eggs in there soon enough."

"Okay Dad," agreed Nina.

"Oh look angel. Doesn't the moon look especially bright this evening?"

Nina looked up and said, "It does." Then another thought came to mind. "Dad when will there be a full moon?"

"I'm not sure, maybe in a week."

"A week!" gasped Nina.

Her reaction seemed out of place. "Is that too soon or too far away?"

"I was just curious how long it takes to get from half-full to full" spurted Nina not knowing what else to say.

"Huh? Okay then," was all Marc said. Nina raced her dad back inside the house in hopes he wouldn't ask anything more about the moon.

<u>Quite the Conundrum</u>

Nina climbed into bed reminding herself that visiting Roo was out of the question. Being responsible for the destruction of her family as she knew it was unthinkable. Nina had come to the conclusion that visiting Gram was the only viable option. Of course, she loved visiting her great-grandma, but the fear of saying a final goodbye to Gram after she died haunted her. Nina had never experienced the death of a loved one or at least while she was old enough to remember it. However, seeing the lingering pain in the eyes of her parents over losing family members was enough of a deterrent.

Sure, there wasn't anything Nina could do to keep her grandma, parents or anyone else from dying, but she could choose to stay away from Gram. That way she wouldn't know when she died. She had no idea when it was that Gram passed and Nina liked it that way. Simply imagining being there when Gram died all but obliterated her heart. Nina clutched at her chest as the thought of

Gram dying caused her heart to ache in a way she'd never experienced. Although Nina and the adult Gram hadn't spent all that much time together they were kindred spirits. Nina also believed it was all the adventures and time in Sovanna with Roo that had solidified their bond. They were the very best of friends. With the knowledge of Roo being Gram as a young girl, it helped to clarify why Nina had felt so close to her from the beginning.

Nina had come to the conclusion that she only had two options. To never again use the music box or to risk one day visiting Gram's house to find it empty or worse to be there when Gram passed. How in the world could she ever make that decision let alone make it in a week? Nina shot up in bed. An idea had broken through the mangled mess of thoughts bombarding her mind and she immediately called out for King Alroi. His voice echoed in her room, making her fearful her parents would hear him, but she asked her question anyway.

With a croaky voice Nina questioned the king, "Could I just use the piano's magic at home? I mean not travel to Sovanna or Gram's, but just play here at home?"

"Smart girl," applauded King Alroi, making Nina feel like she had found a way out of such an impossible decision, but his next words destroyed her hope. "You are very wise to consider that as an option, but it is no longer possible. Once you've repeatedly traveled through portals into other magical worlds the music box will default to those locations."

With King Alroi's last words still hanging in the air Nina found herself once again in front of his throne. He didn't waste any time explaining things further. "I have your Gram's magical necklace because she gave it to me. She knew it was far too dangerous for her to hold onto the key leading to her magical world, while you also had a key to Sovanna. Surrendering her necklace made the pathway into her world unpassable no matter how hard the piano tried to find the entrance. The only door the music box key could open was to

Sovanna, leaving you to play with Roo. Never the two shall meet," stressed King Alroi before continuing, "That is why she said goodbye to you. Your Gram didn't want to risk losing you as her granddaughter. She made the choice for you to visit her as a child, never considering you would discover who Roo truly was."

The king's explanation helped Nina understand why her Gram had said goodbye, but Nina's heart still ached from that surprising farewell. "So without Gram having her key I can't get in?"

"That is correct. The piano is unable to locate the portal to her now that she no longer holds the key," reiterated the king.

Nina found herself back in her bed with her mouth half-opened, as she was about to ask the king several more questions. There was so much more she didn't understand. Whether by magic or pure fatigue Nina fell fast asleep. She awoke feeling ready for school. Nina hoped it would be a distraction from her impending decision and the weighty sensation in her heart. It did the trick. By the time Nina arrived home from school she was feeling like her old self. Like she was before she knew anything about the magical piano and all that comes with it. Part of her wished she didn't have such a wonderful imagination. Nina had once thought it sad her grandma and mom never experienced the magical world of Sovanna, which she'd been granted permission to visit, but now she was starting to think they got off easy.

Valerie peeked into Nina's room to find her staring at the piano. "Here let me wind it for you," Valerie offered picking up the music box and winding it up before Nina could stop her. Thankfully Valerie didn't notice the panicked look in her daughter's eyes before she turned to leave. As the beautiful song began to play Nina realized just how much she missed hearing the melody.

"Hello dear one," greeted Tarak.

Nina crouched down in the tall grass. "I can't be here. Please send me home," she whispered.

"You are safe. Roo is no longer here."

Nina was terrified by Tarak's words. "Where is she?" demanded Nina.

Tarak extended undeserved favor to Nina and answered, "King Alroi has immensely extended Sovanna and Roo is off exploring it as we speak. She's been gone for days."

It wasn't until that precise moment did Nina realize she had absolutely finalized her decision on seeing Roo. Eliminating the lives of her family was far more than she could bear. In a resounding tone Nina exclaimed, "I will not be visiting Roo or Sovanna ever again."

"And for your final decision?" inquired King Alroi.

He had done it again. Nina and Tarak were in the king's kingdom, only this time the three of them were standing high on a cliff. The majestic castle hung in midair and as it rotated Nina was more and more impressed with the magnificent splendor of it. Tarak cleared his throat reminding Nina she hadn't answered the king. "Don't I have a few more days?" questioned an alarmed Nina finally noticing the king was closer to human size.

"You do," King Alroi confirmed, but the look in his eyes revealed he knew she had already made her final decision. "I will give you the allotted time if that is your wish."

Clearly getting anything passed King Alroi was out of the question and Nina wondered if he perceived what her choice would be before she did. Nina spoke from the heart, "I wish to visit with Gram for as long as she lives."

"Welcome back!" Gram cheered joyfully.

Nina felt loved and safe in her Gram's arms. The smell of cookies baking in the oven only added another layer to the lovely moment. Nina's tear filled eyes made it hard to see Gram's face clearly. It was the first-time Nina understood the phrase, "Happy tears." Hanging from Gram's neck was her necklace. "King Alroi gave you back your necklace," Nina pointed out.

"Yes he did," answered Gram placing her hand over the pendant with appreciation radiating in her eyes.

"Isn't that dangerous?"

"No, now that you've made your decision it's safe for me to wear it. Your decision has locked the piano on a single magical course. There aren't any other paths for it to take."

Gram went on to explain how Nina's decision had the same result as when Gram gave King Alroi her necklace. When Gram finished unraveling the tangled web of questions in her great-granddaughter's mind Nina said, "So by giving King Alroi my decision not to visit Roo he was able to lock the gateway to Sovanna?"

"Yes, but it had to be your choice not his, just like when I gave him my necklace. That was my choice and my choice alone." Gram's face expressed gratitude, so much so that her eyes filled with tears. It took a moment for her to gather her emotions and when she did Nina was astonished by her words. "King Alroi is a righteous, compassionate and honorable king. In his kindness, he has granted you the privilege of using the piano at home."

Nina couldn't get the words out fast enough, "So I can still play with Crackers and my other toys at home?"

"Yes sweets. The piano will honor your wishes for magical playtime at home when you tell it to 'Play me a tale,' just like you used to."

What a wonderful turn of events. Nina was certain her magical adventures at home had come to an end. The king had basically told her that. When she made her decision to only visit Gram she was confident that had only solidified that fact, but thankfully she was wrong. Beaming with excitement Nina said, "Yay!!! 'Play me a tale' means I can have magical adventures at home, but what do I say when I want to come here?"

"Just focus on me when the music starts. There's no need to say anything."

Nina wanted clarification to ensure nothing bad would happen. The last several days were proof there was far more to magic than she knew. "It's that simple?" asked a skeptical Nina.

"It's that simple," answered Gram tenderly locking eyes with her great-granddaughter. The

330

pure love and reassurance in Gram's eyes eased Nina's remaining fears. No sooner did Gram pull the freshly baked cookies from the oven did Tiger join them as if on cue. "Gingersnaps. My favorite," announced Tiger while rubbing on Nina's leg begging to be petted. Nina picked him up and nuzzled the cat making him purr. Together they shared ice cold milk and more cookies than any of them should have eaten. Gram put the rest of the cookies in her cookie jar, which was just about at its limit. She clearly had been very busy baking. The three of them moved to the living room where Nina found pictures scattered over the coffee table and floor. It reminded her of discovering the truth about Roo, which made her stomach jump and knot up.

"Don't worry Nina all is well," coaxed Gram. "As a matter-of-fact we're going to have so much fun with this."

Tiger asked, "Can I come too?"

"If you would like," responded Gram before choosing a picture of herself at a circus. In the photo a much younger Gram was holding a paper cone with a large ball of cotton candy on it. Gram faced Nina with the picture in one hand, then taking hold of one of her great-granddaughters hands she asked, "Shall we?" Before Nina could answer she felt her body tingle like never before and in disbelief she watched herself go head first into the photo.

It all happened so quickly. Nina didn't remember seeing or hearing anything as she was sucked into the old black and white print, but she now found herself at the circus. Holding her hand was Gram, but younger like she was in the picture. "Gram?" questioned Nina in a hushed voice. Terrified that her appearance at the circus and using the term Gram would have devastating effects on both their lives.

"It's quite all right Nina. I'm still here I just look like I did in the photo," assured Gram before Tiger pointed out he still looked the same and that he and Gram travel back and forth in time on a regular basis via her pictures. The one thing that stood out and gave Nina the creeps was they were all colorless.

"It looks so weird here," moaned Nina.

Gram giggled and said, "Oh I forgot you're not used to black and white photos let alone being in one." Gram placed her right hand on her left shoulder and said, "Watch this." She then moved her arm to right as far as she could reach while wiggling her fingers. Colors appeared to be trickling from Gram's hand. Nina was amazed to see everything come to life as the colors washed over them and their surroundings.

"That's so cool," cheered Nina watching the bland environment around her become vividly bright. The red and white circus tent with its golden trim was center stage. Surrounding the huge tent were vendors selling popcorn, cotton candy, balloons and so much more. Two carousels flanked the main tent's entrance, one with exquisitely painted horses and the other with all sorts of wild animals from an elephant to a jackrabbit. Laughter caught Nina's attention helping her spot a gigantic Ferris wheel full of children having a wonderful time.

"What would you like to do first?" asked Gram bringing Nina's attention back to her.

"The Ferris wheel!" replied Nina jumping up and down. She had always wanted to ride one.

After the Ferris wheel, they rode each of the carousels, ate some cotton candy then headed into the fun house. Upon their exit from the fun house they heard the ringmaster shout out that the circus's main attraction was about to begin. Nina couldn't get inside the tent fast enough. She had never been to a circus. Nina was filled with wonderment as the trapeze artists defied gravity with their acrobatic skills. The clowns made her laugh until her belly hurt and the wild animal performances were more than impressive, but it was the equestrian stunts that won her over. Riding a horse had always been a dream of Nina's; however, these riders weren't just riding the horses. In long flowing gowns the women stood on the horses as they made their way around the tent. When they reached the center ring they moved in a dance-like fashion changing from one formation to the next as the band played.

Just when Nina believed it couldn't get any better it did. The group of riders filed out of the ring and no sooner had they disappeared out of sight in ran a light brown horse with a black mane and tail. Nina thought the horse had gotten lose as she didn't see a rider. When the horse made its way around the ring Nina noticed a woman hanging upside down from one of her legs. The lady wore a bright purple and gold long sleeve pant suit. The rhinestones on her one-piece costume sparkled as she moved. In amazement Nina watch as the rider's hands almost touched the dirt floor and her other leg was extended alongside the horse's neck. Not once did the lady sit properly in the saddle. She hung off one side of the horse then the other in various positions and stood on the horse's back as it sped around the ring. The big finale was the woman standing on the back of two different horses while waving a large flag overhead. All the other performers filed in and surrounded the ring before taking their bows.

The crowd erupted in applause. Rising to their feet the crowd kept cheering and clapping until the only person left was the ringmaster who wished them all a wonderful night. As Nina, Gram and Tiger headed out of the tent they walked straight into Gram's kitchen. "Will I ever get used to that?" questioned Nina feeling a little wobbly on her feet.

"You will," Gram assured her before telling her she needed to get back home.

Lost in the magical time with Gram helped Nina forget the complications and dangers of time travel, at least for a while. "I thought if I went back in time that would change everything," Nina pointed out, fearful her circus trip may have caused irreversible damage to her world. Was Gram putting Nina's life and the rest of her family at risk of never being born? She couldn't help but ask, "Did going to the circus when you were younger...."

Gram interrupted, "Please calm down Nina. I don't have all the answers, but I can tell you that I'm able to visit places and times through my photo's without causing a ripple effect in time. I don't quite understand it myself, but it is wonderful. None of my adventures have ever resulted in a time paradox nor have I ever been warned against my travels. Quite the contrary. I've been encouraged to not only do as much time traveling as I wish, but to fully appreciate the incredibly magical gift I've been given."

"How long have you been doing that?"

"Ever since I received the piano. It's always been a part of my magical journeys, but never before have I been able to share it with a family member or friend," beamed Gram whose teary eyes expressed her jubilation over this new development. "Nina you have made one of my most earnest wishes come true. Thank you so much sweets," expressed Gram giving her a huge bear hug.

Nina wanted to believe what Gram was telling her but part of her was still afraid of the possible consequences. After returning home Nina snuck into her parent's room to find both her mom and dad asleep in their bed. She also checked on the nursery. Everything was at it should be, not a single thing was out of place. Feeling all was well Nina went to her room and climbed into bed. Her visit with Gram had been a dream come true and the real world was left unchanged allowing her to relax enough to drift off to a peaceful night's sleep.

Intricate Matters

To be on the safe side Nina remained at home whenever she used the music box. Anytime she wound up the piano and said those magic words, "Play me a tale," Nina would remain unwavering in her focus on her bedroom. Her steadfast determination had consistently worked. As the weeks passed her concern over having changed important events in time faded away. Nina grew confident in Gram's words and began to accept the fact of it being safe to travel through her old pictures. She knew Gram wouldn't intentionally lie to her, but perhaps there was something Gram didn't know and Nina wasn't ready to chance it. At least not yet.

A few weekends later Nina decided it was time to go see Gram. Simply thinking about visiting Gram made Nina smile making it extremely easy to stay focused on her. Before the music box could finish a chord of notes she found herself sitting on Gram's couch.

"Welcome back sweets," greeted Gram, giving Nina one of her lasting hugs. "It's been too long since your last visit."

Nina turned her head so she could breathe as Gram held her tight to her chest. The strong scent of Gram's favorite perfume overwhelmed Nina. She didn't know the name of the perfume, but it reminded Nina of the time she went with her mom to a flower shop. Never before had Nina seen or smelt so may flowers at one time. Grandma smelled very much like that store with its over abundant floral displays.

"Would you let me show you something?" asked Gram tentatively. Nina nodded in agreement.

Gram walked over to the fireplace mantle and brought back a wooden box carved with leaf covered vines on the lid. Before opening the box, she took a deep breath and smiled at Nina. Opening the top revealed colored pictures unlike the ones strewn all over Grams living room. "This is how I knew who you were," stated Gram lifting a picture of Nina in her mom's arms at the hospital where she was born. Then Gram showed Nina more photos of her parents, grandma and other family members.

"I don't understand, those pictures are in albums at my house. How did you get them?"

"One day this box appeared on the mantle. It was empty and I had no idea where it came from, but living with magic all my life I felt there must have been a reason for its arrival. In a little over a month I received an answer. The picture of your mom holding you in the hospital with your full name and date of birth written on the back showed up. After that other pictures started coming, each one with the names and location listed on the back. I would get at least one a day in the very beginning, then it tapered off to a new photo every once in a while. In time, I was able to not only piece together the family, but I got to watch each of you grow over the years."

Nina could hardly believe her eyes. Gram seemed to be defying all the rules of time travel if not magic itself. "What does this mean?"

Confidently Gram replied, "It means we can have all the adventures we want. Not only can we venture into my old pictures we can travel through a painting or drawing and with that Gram took Nina's hand pulling her towards the large landscape painting above her fireplace. Standing in a large meadow filled with an abundance of flowers Nina noticed they were nestled in a valley surrounded by rolling green hills. There were blossoming trees scattered about with either white or pink flowers and a lazy river meandered through the landscape. A sweet fragrance filled the air as the blooms blew in a gentle breeze. The massive number of assorted flowers varied in colors, shapes and sizes. Nina found herself sniffing a bright purple flower that was actually lots of tiny flowers bunched together in a way that resembled the cotton candy Gram had at the circus.

"I so enjoy this spot," admitted Gram bending over to smell a bright red rose.

"It's beautiful," agreed Nina. Then something Gram had mentioned before going into the painting came to the forefront of Nina's mind. "If we can go into a drawing like we did this painting does that mean we can draw a mermaid village or something else and go there?"

"It does," beamed Gram as she took Nina's hand sending them back to Gram's living room.

"Would you like to play with Roo?"

"I can't," stressed Nina afraid her fears about magic were about to become reality.

"You are right, you can't play with Roo from Sovanna, but we can go into a photo of me when I'm young and let our imaginations go wild and see where it takes us."

This was far too tempting. Nina whispered, "Okay, show me." When Gram and Nina arrived at what must have been the house Gram grew up in Nina's eyes opened wide at the sight of Roo standing next to her still holding her hand. "Gram is that you?" asked Nina watching their surroundings shift into color.

"It is, but just like the circus picture made me look younger, this picture makes me look like I did as a girl. What do you think?" Gram asked looking and sounding just like the Roo Nina remembered.

"I think that's amazing!" replied a thrilled Nina before hugging Roo as tightly as she could. Nina couldn't believe she had the best of both worlds. Not only could she play and go on adventures with her very best friend Roo, she could spend time with Gram as an adult learning how to do all sorts of things. Worrying about how or when Gram would die was all but forgotten. Nina had every intention of enjoying all the time she could with Gram.

Seeing Roo again reminded Nina of the Valentine card in her sock drawer. Roo was about the same age as she was at the ranch so this was perfect. Next time Nina dropped by she would bring the card and revisit the specific picture they were in.

Noticing Nina's distracted look Roo asked, "Do you have any other questions before you go home?"

"I have to go?" asked a disappointed Nina without answering Roo's actual question.

"Yes, but we will have lots more fun soon," nodded Roo sounding once again like she did in Sovanna which took Nina back to those fond memories.

Nina remained both ecstatic and bewildered at being able to spend time with Gram as an adult and child. She couldn't quite wrap her mind around it. Then a thought hit her, "Can we travel through the pictures in the wooden box?"

"No. I am not allowed to use those pictures for adventures. That was explicitly and repeatedly told to me once I received the first picture."

Part of Nina wanted to ask Gram if she had ever tried, but inside her heart something told her even wondering about that could harm Gram and the rest of her family. Clearly Nina's intense look gave away her dilemma. Gram confessed she once thought about defying the directive she'd been given. The simple act of even considering going into the pictures held in the carved wooden box, resulted in the disappearance of the cherished gift. Nina asked, "When did you get the box back?"

"It came back over a year later. I repeatedly apologized for considering traveling into the pictures; although, at the time I wasn't sure who or what I was apologizing to. Either way after a year of expressing my regret the box returned," uttered Gram with dismay and a tinge of unease in her eyes. It was clear that experience brought back harsh memories for her.

Nina rushed into Gram's arms and with a hug and a kiss Nina returned home filled with both renewed excitement of what was to come and a heightened respect for the boundaries of magic. Gram may not have known back then it was King Alroi she was apologizing to, but Nina was certain it had to be him. Hearing about the punishment Gram was given for merely thinking about using magic on the gifted box of pictures sent a chill up Nina's back. She would never admit it to Gram, but she was actually shocked King Alroi had returned the gift to her. His esteemed presence alone demanded respect and Nina knew better than to test his authority. She was confident the tenderness in his eyes would be replaced with fierce intensity if he were ever deliberately disobeyed. Having been taught that actions have consequences Nina could only imagine what intentionally defying King Alroi's instructions would bring. There was no doubt that the magic from her life and Gram's would be eliminated at the very least.

No sooner was Nina back at home did she pull Roo's Valentine card from her sock drawer. In order to keep from forgetting the card the next time she visited Gram, Nina leaned the card against the music box and smiled with anticipation.

Much to Nina's surprise and delight she would be back at Gram's before bedtime. The amazement Nina felt whenever the music box wound itself up had not faded over time. The clicking sound of the winding key clued Nina in. She quickly grabbed the Valentine card, hid it behind her back and thought of Gram.

"Back so soon?"

Nina smiled with glee, "Yes, can we go back into the photo we used last time to see Roo?"

"Of course," Gram agreed while searching for the picture. "Here it is."

In a split-second Nina was once again with Roo and it wasn't until that moment did Nina wonder what month it was. Giving Roo a Valentine's Day card during the wrong time of the year made no sense and it might confuse her. Or would it? After all, it was Gram. Time travel was becoming extremely perplexing.

Suddenly the world they were in began to blur and spin until it became a garbled mess of images. Covering her face with her hands Nina struggled to regain her balance. When she felt better and looked around she noticed Valentine decorations in Roo's house. Somehow the surroundings of the picture they entered had moved to February. Roo called for Nina to join her outside in the backyard.

Nina managed to find her way to the backyard, but she couldn't locate Roo in the wide-open space before her. "Where are you?"

"I'm up here in my tree house," shouted Roo waving through a small window.

Nina raced towards the tree house, put the Valentine card in between her teeth and climbed up the steep stairs, which were much more like a ladder than steps. Taking a moment to enjoy the view from the tree house deck prompted Roo to hurry her along. Nina went through the arched doorway and spotted pink streamers, red balloons and heart shaped cookies on a tiny table.

Roo greeted Nina with excitement, "Happy Valentine's Day!"

"Happy Valentine's Day to you too," cheered Nina now offering Roo her card.

After taking the card and saying a quick thank you Roo tore the envelope opened and with wide eyes looked at the beautifully printed card. The images were crisp and clear. "I've never seen such a pretty card before," that's when Roo's smile turned into a bit of a frown. Reluctantly Roo handed Nina her Valentine's Day card. "I hope you like it," mumbled Roo looking ashamed.

Nina didn't understand what was happening so she tried to make Roo smile, "I'm sure I'll love it." Nina carefully opened the envelope and pulled the square card from it. On the front sat a young girl with dark braids holding a heart that said "For my Friend." The girl's blue dress and hair ribbon had red swirls on them which perfectly matched the red heart sitting above the girl's head with the words "A Valentine," on it. Nina reread the card out loud, "A Valentine for my friend." Her voice rang of happiness and looking Roo dead in her eyes Nina announced, "It's the most beautiful Valentine card I've ever gotten."

Roo seemed unconvinced and appeared to be expressing regret, "I'm glad you like it, but I'm sorry it's not as pretty as yours."

"Why would you say that?" asked a bewildered Nina.

"Mine is on thin floppy paper and is a messy sketch with faded colors. The card you gave....."

Nina couldn't help but interrupt. "Roo, I've never received a card like this one. It's the most unique and special Valentine's card I've ever gotten and best of all it's from you. I really do love it, thank you again."

That seemed to have done the trick. Roo hugged Nina tightly then offered her some cookies and milk. The girls ate so much their bellies hurt, then they played checkers, dolls and hop scotch. Playing with Roo was a dream come true. As the sun fell behind the large trees Nina knew it was time to go. "I guess I should get home," and no sooner had Nina stated that did the world around her morph back into a distorted mess before placing them back into the photo's original environment. Then back to Gram's house and home with barely enough time to exchange goodbyes.

Nina shook her head in an effort to clear her mind. Standing in her bedroom felt more like a dream than being with Gram or Roo. Was she losing her grasp on reality? Perhaps she needed to spend more time at home between her magical trips. No matter how much she loved her magical experiences it was her family and the real world that she loved most of all. No magic could replace her parents, grandma or the sibling she had yet to meet.

There was also one other thing she wondered about. How did she and Roo land on Valentine's Day in Gram's picture? The strange way everything changed from one place in time to the exact date Nina wanted was more than a little disturbing.

King Alroi came to mind. Nina wasn't sure how or why he would help her spend Valentine's Day with Roo, but Nina couldn't find another explanation. The king had to be the one who orchestrated it all. That's when a familiar voice rang in Nina's ears. There was only one creature with such an endearing and sweet-sounding voice. Nina turned around and confirmed it was Sunnee fluttering around her room.

"Hello Sunnee. What are you doing here?" questioned Nina lifting her hand and allowing the beautiful butterfly to land on her index finger.

"I have a message from King Alroi."

Nina's heart skipped a beat. Had she done something wrong? Hesitantly she asked, "What's the message."

"The king wants me to tell you to trust in his magic. He has been doing this for a very very long time. Your visits to Gram and her collection of magical pictures are safe from danger. Each and every picture the King has duplicated for her from your albums has been magically created. They all have been positioned in a specific section of time. Some are stuck in a single day; others can move about in a particular year and a select few can navigate through an entire decade."

"Except the ones in Gram's wooden box," stated Nina in an effort to make sure the king knew she understood the rules.

"Yes, except for those. Which is why you've both been commanded not to ever use those for time travel. There are serious repercussions for using or even pondering that course of action. King Alroi simply wants you to have fun, abide by the rules and stop questioning everything."

Feeling confident in knowing the dangers Nina blurted, "We could destroy our family." Nina couldn't help herself and asked, "But what if I accidentally break a rule? Or..."

Sunnee's sweet voice took on a serious tone, "You know the rules and there's no way to 'accidentally' break a rule. Choosing to break a rule is a deliberate act of defiance. As long as you remember that, you won't ever be in danger."

Nina knew that truth all too well. Anytime she had broken a rule at home she was reminded of how she deliberately chose to do so. Whatever the reason was for breaking the rule she was ultimately accepting the risk of getting caught. Which usually happened, leading to consequences for her misbehavior. Remnants of Nina's artwork done with permanent marker on her bedroom wall remain to this day. No matter how long or hard she scrubbed, she couldn't get all of it off. The sections that are still partially visible serve as a constant reminder of how miserable consequences can be. Nina confessed, "I know, my mom and dad tell me the same thing when I've done something wrong."

"Then don't break any rules," declared Sunnee, stating the obvious.

The following morning Nina was up and ready for school before Valerie came in to wake her up. With time to spare Nina played in her room then a thought came to her. She rushed to the nursery and ran to the crib. Peering inside the empty crib Nina's mind wandered and imagined all the magical adventures she would someday share with her sibling. As far as Nina was concerned life couldn't get any better. She had a brother or a sister on the way, a magical secret that was far beyond anything even her exceptional imagination could have dreamt up and her family was still intact.

As Nina left the nursery with a heart full of love, thankfulness and anticipation she whispered, "Thank you King Alroi." She wasn't sure how he would hear her but she was convinced he did.

King Alroi smiled over hearing Nina's words of gratitude, but primarily for her believing so strongly in magic. The king stepped back and admired the golden framed photos on the wall. Above the rather small number of mounted pictures was an oversized rectangular piece of wood. Beautifully inscribed into the wood were the words, "Magical Forevermore," in an overly elaborate cursive. King Alroi focused on Gram's photo and he watched her reminiscing over her day with Nina. He envisioned how wonderful it would be if Nina could someday have her own picture on this distinctive wall. If her imagination lived on like Gram's had Nina too would be honored.

There was a clear distinction between those who lost their belief in magic and those rare individuals who for the remainder of their lives held onto their childlike ingenuity. The latter were few and far between, but when one of those uniquely gifted children grew into an even more innovative adult, King Alroi would reward their uncommon belief. He would happily and proudly hang their photo in this remarkable and cherished one-of-a-kind room.

An honored space dedicated to preserving the magic for those who refused to let it fade from their lives. King Alroi grinned as he left the room.

After making sure to lock the door, he blew on the key he held in his hand causing it to disperse into a golden cloud of shimmering dust. Each nearly microscopic piece returned to its shrouded hiding place. No one except King Alroi could bring the multimillions of key fragments back together. He alone knew how to do so. As an added layer of protection, the key particles would only listen to his voice. King Alroi was the epitome of magic.

Author's Note

Thank you to all my readers. Whether you purchased an eBook or a paperback copy I truly appreciate your business. "Play Me a Tale" is the first of my books to be available in paperback which is very exciting.

Please take the time to rate and/or review "Play Me a Tale" when you've finished the story. Your rating and/or review of my books are a huge help in getting them noticed by the masses. I also would like to thank any of you who recommend my books to family and friends.

Remember to follow me on Amazon and/or Goodreads. You can also subscribe to my free monthly newsletter by emailing me at email@tl-stevens.com and letting me know you would like to join the group.

www.tl-stevens.com